THE QUIET DIVIDE

GABY ORON

www.astraechoes.co.uk

All rights reserved.
Text © Gaby Oron, 2026
Cover and interior design © Gaby Oron, 2026

First published in the United Kingdom, 2026

No part of this publication may be reproduced, stored in a retrieval system, or transmitted in any form, by any means (electronic, mechanical, photocopying, recording, or otherwise) without the prior written permission of the author.

978-1-9191806-0-1 – Print Edition
978-1-9191806-1-8 – eBook Edition

This is a work of fiction.
Names, characters, places, incidents and dialogues are either products of the author's imagination or are used fictitiously.
Any resemblance to actual people, living or dead, events, or locales is purely coincidental.

Contents

1. Event Horizon — 3
2. Echoes in the Blood — 10
3. The Shape of What's Coming — 19
4. Glass in the Veins — 34
5. All That We Leave Unsaid — 42
6. The Weight of Knowing — 53
7. Between the Sparks & Silence — 69
8. By the Book — 88
9. All Stations Failing — 108
10. Born Into the Fire — 125
11. The Quiet Divide — 134

The Quiet Divide

"There are only two ways to live your life. One is as though nothing is a miracle. The other is as though everything is a miracle."

— **Albert Einstein**

2597
Meridian Station

1

Event Horizon

Cira watched the containment readings fluctuate in a pattern she'd never seen before. The numbers blinked amber on her tablet—not quite in alarm territory, but definitely not normal. After eight years of working with deorum ore, she'd developed an intuition for its behaviour, and right now, every instinct told her something was wrong.

"Dalen, are you seeing this?" She kept her voice level despite the tightness in her chest.

Across Meridian Station's monitoring bay, Dalen straightened from his console. "Third spike in the last hour." He tapped a sequence into his console, pulling up additional data streams. "Maintenance claims it's calibration issues, but these harmonics don't match any calibration pattern I've ever seen."

Cira swiped through the data, unconvinced. "I don't like this. The refinery was never meant to handle this much raw ore at once."

Dalen's eyes met hers. "That was Praetorium's decision, not ours. They wanted faster production."

"And we wanted safety protocols, god damn it." She shook her head. "I'm tempted to just pull the plug on this."

Dalen's expression softened momentarily. "Come on, we both know you don't mean that, you know what we're doing with the deorum ore—this could change everything."

"If it doesn't kill us first." Cira stood, smoothing her grey lab coat. "I'm going down there. Whatever is happening, it doesn't look good."

Dalen looked up, his expression shifting from professional concern to something more personal. "Protocol says remote diagnostics first."

"Protocol wasn't written for harmonics like these." She was already moving toward the door. "Look, it'll be fine, just keep an eye on Bay Four. If the containment field drops below ninety-two per cent, call Kat."

The corridor outside the monitoring bay hummed with the constant drone of air recyclers. Meridian wasn't a luxury station; it was functional, industrial, and perpetually understaffed. Cira passed two maintenance workers arguing over part allocation as she approached the lift. She nodded to the security officer, but didn't recognise him.

Must've come in on the last rotation.

"Heading down to processing," she said, swiping her access card.

The guard—Jameson, according to his badge—raised an eyebrow. "Thought that was off-limits during extraction."

"It is normally, but I need to know if what we are seeing is because of a calibration issue or not, and I can't do that from up there." She offered a tight smile. "Just a quick check on the readings."

"Your funeral." He shrugged.

The lift descended with a groan that never failed to make her nervous. Meridian had been built quickly, corners cut where deemed acceptable. The result was a station that worked—mostly—but every day managed to remind its inhabitants of its fragility in a hundred small ways.

The processing level was eerily quiet compared to the usual hum of activity. Extraction cycles were typically all noise and movement—technicians monitoring equipment, engineers making adjustments, the mechanical symphony of machinery refining deorum ore into something else. Something that might change the trajectory of Sacramentum. Today, the automated systems worked alone, the observation room empty except for a single technician who looked up with surprise as Cira entered.

"Dr. Cira? You're not supposed to be down here during active extraction."

"I know Mills. Just checking something." She moved to the main console, bringing up the same readings she'd been monitoring upstairs. They looked worse here, closer to the source. "Have you noticed anything unusual with the harmonic stabilisers?"

Mills shrugged, returning to his game on a personal device. "Above my pay grade. I just watch for red lights."

Cira bit back a retort. She'd worked her way up from positions like his, and the culture of minimal effort still frustrated her. Eight years at Meridian, and she still hadn't adjusted to the Praetorium way. Katrina understood—they'd often shared their frustrations over late-night coffee in the lab, planning improvements that would inevitably end up not happening due to funding.

The observation window provided a view into the processing chamber itself—a cavernous room dominated by the containment cylinder at its centre. Inside, raw deorum ore floated in a magnetically controlled suspension, pulsing with a characteristic yellow glow as extraction beams refined the valuable particles. It was beautiful, in its way, this substance that defied conventional physics.

The readout on the console beeped, drawing her attention back. The harmonic resonance had spiked again, higher this time. She opened a direct channel to Dalen.

"These readings are definitely not calibration issues. The ore is destabilising at the molecular level."

Dalen's voice came through with a burst of static. "How bad?"

She studied the numbers, unease growing. "Bad enough that we should pause the refinement cycle. I'm going to call Kat."

"Wait—" His voice cut through sharper now. "The system logs show something strange. Someone accessed the extraction parameters last night."

Cira frowned. "That's impossible. Kat locked down those systems herself after the last audit."

"Nevertheless, someone got in. Give me two minutes."

She turned back to the observation window, studying the containment cylinder. The yellow glow had intensified, pulsing in an irregular rhythm that made her eyes hurt to follow. Something was definitely wrong.

"Mills, when was the last full diagnostic run on the containment field?"

The technician looked up, annoyance clear on his face. "Yesterday. Standard procedure."

"And the results?"

"Green across the board. Look, if you're worried, call Director Wright. I'm just here to monitor."

The console beeped again, more urgently this time. Cira turned to see the numbers shifting from amber to red. The containment field was fluctuating wildly now, dropping to eighty-nine per cent before bouncing back to ninety-four.

She hit the comm again. "Dalen, we're losing stability. I'm calling Kat now."

"Hold off!" Alarm edged his voice. "The beam intensity is fifteen per cent above safety parameters. If I bring that back down, we should be fine.'

"Fifteen?" Cira felt her stomach drop. "That's well beyond safety margins for this grade of ore."

"I know. I'm trying to override, but the system is locked with credentials I don't have."

Cira was already moving, heading for the emergency shutdown panel on the far wall. "I'm initiating manual shutdown."

She never made it. A high-pitched whine filled the air, rising rapidly in pitch until it hurt her ears. Through the observation window, she observed the deorum ore in the containment cylinder begin to spin faster, the yellow glow brightening to a painful intensity.

"Mills, emergency protocols! Now!" She said, but the technician was already bolting for the door.

The console erupted in alarms. The containment field was failing, dropping past critical thresholds faster than the system could compensate. Cira slammed her hand on the station-wide alert, triggering klaxons throughout Meridian.

"Dalen!" She shouted into her comm. "Evacuate the monitoring bay! Get everyone out of the adjacent sections!"

His response was lost in a burst of static as the first shock wave hit. The observation window cracked, a spiderweb of fractures spreading across its surface. Cira dove for cover behind a support column as the window shattered inward, showering the room with transparent polymer shards.

The second wave knocked her off her feet. The lights flickered and died, the room now lit solely by the glowing ore. Through the broken window, she could see the containment cylinder itself beginning to fracture, yellow-white energy spilling out in crackling arcs.

She needed to move. Now.

Cira scrambled to her feet, stumbling toward the exit as the station shuddered around her. The door to the corridor was jammed halfway open, almost not leaving enough space to squeeze through. She forced herself into the gap, ignoring the sharp edge cutting into her lab coat.

The corridor beyond was chaos—emergency lights strobing, evacuation sirens blaring, and the distant sound of shouting. She turned toward the emergency shelter, only to be thrown against the wall as another explosion rocked the station.

Behind her, the containment cylinder ruptured. A blinding flash of yellow-white light erupted outward, followed by a wave of energy that distorted the air around her.

There was nowhere to run. The wave hit her full force, knocking her unconscious as energy washed over her body.

Her last thought before darkness claimed her was of Dalen, and whether she'd sent him to his death.

2

ECHOES IN THE BLOOD

Cira closed her eyes, the throbbing in her head a relentless drum. And in the darkness, there was light. Not a memory, but a feeling—a sense of being unspooled and rewoven on a golden loom. She could see shapes, clothed in fur and starlight, their eyes holding echoes of what was and what would be. They danced a design of becoming, and at its centre, a single mote of life ignited. A voice that was not a voice whispered in her mind:

Divided shall be made whole.

She gasped, her eyes flying open, the antiseptic smell of the med bay a shocking return to reality.

"Easy there." The voice belonged to Dr. Brown, Meridian's chief medical officer. "You've had quite an experience."

Memory returned in fragments—the destabilising deorum ore, the alarms, the containment breach. She bolted upright despite the doctor's protests.

"Dalen—is he—"

"He's fine." Dr. Brown adjusted something on her IV. "Minor injuries. He's been in to see you twice already."

Relief washed over her, followed immediately by more questions. "How long have I been out?"

"Almost thirty hours." The doctor checked her pupils with a small light. "You were directly exposed to the energy released when the containment failed. We weren't sure what to expect."

Thirty hours. Cira tried to process this as she took in her surroundings. The medical bay was busier than she'd ever seen it—every bed occupied, medical staff moving between patients.

"How many were hurt?"

Dr. Brown's expression tightened. "Fourteen injured, mostly minor. Three critical." A pause. "Two dead."

It took her a moment to process what she heard. "Who?"

"Mills and Santos. They were closest to the containment cylinder when it ruptured."

Mills. The technician who'd been playing games when she arrived. Who'd run for the door when the alarms started. Guilt twisted in her stomach.

"What about the station? How bad is the damage?"

"Processing level two is completely destroyed. Adjacent sections suffered structural damage." The doctor's voice was clinical, detached. "Director Wright can fill you in on the details. She's been asking about you."

As if summoned by her name, Katrina appeared in the doorway. Tall and imposing even in standard station attire, Meridian's director carried herself with the quiet intensity of someone who'd built her career on authority and calculated risk. Today, however, her usual composure seemed strained, dark circles visible beneath her eyes.

"Doctor. I need a moment with Cira"

Dr. Brown nodded. "Five minutes. She needs rest."

When they were alone, Katrina moved closer to the bed, her expression softening. "Jesus Cira, what happened down there?"

"Someone had been in the system, Kat, they'd been tampering with the extraction parameters," Cira said, her arms trembling beneath her weight, collapsing as she struggled to rise from the bed.

"Ok, ok, like the Doc said, rest for now, the main thing you're both all right."

Cira blinked in confusion. "Both?"

Katrina's eyes gravitated to Cira's midsection. "You and the baby. Dr. Brown detected elevated hCG levels during your initial blood work. You should've told me you were pregnant."

"Baby?" Cira's voice came out as a strangled whisper. She gripped the edge of the bed, her knuckles turning white. "That's not possible."

Katrina frowned. "The tests were quite clear. You're definitely pregnant."

"No, you don't understand." Cira shook her head, her heart hammering against her ribs. "I can't get pregnant. The doctors on Sacramentum confirmed it years ago, after the complications with the first pregnancy."

A cold wave of shock washed over her. She'd made peace with this notion long ago—had built her life around her work instead, accepting that some things, like having a second child, weren't meant to be. She and Dalen had discussed adoption, but with their schedules at Meridian, they'd put it off.

"How did Brown even test for that?" she asked, her voice unsteady. "It's not standard protocol for accident victims."

"Your blood work showed anomalies. He was being thorough." Katrina studied her face. "You didn't know?"

"How could I?" Cira pressed a trembling hand to her abdomen. "It's medically impossible."

Or it had been.

"We'll need to monitor you. Your exposure during the accident complicates matters."

Cira forced herself to focus, to push past the shock.

"What do you remember about the accident?"

The abrupt change of subject seemed to catch Cira off guard. "The ore was destabilising. Harmonic resonance was off the charts. Like I said, Dalen found that someone had accessed the extraction parameters."

Katrina's expression didn't change, but something flickered in her eyes. "Yes, we've identified the access point. A security breach during routine maintenance."

"That doesn't make sense." Cira shook her head, wincing at the pain the movement caused. "Those systems have redundant safeguards. One person couldn't accidentally override them."

"It wasn't accidental." Katrina's voice dropped even lower. "The modifications were deliberate—targeted at destabilising the ore during peak extraction."

Cira stared at her. "Sabotage? Who would—"

"That's what I need to find out." Katrina glanced toward the door, ensuring they were still alone. "Listen carefully, Cira. Praetorium has already dispatched a security team. They'll be here in three days. Until then, all information about the accident is classified. No communications off-station. No discussions with anyone not involved in the cleanup."

Cira felt a chill that had nothing to do with the medical bay's temperature. "You think this goes beyond Meridian."

"I know it does." Katrina's intensity was almost palpable. "The only people with clearance to modify those parameters are me, you, and three executives at Praetorium headquarters. This wasn't random vandalism."

"Two people are dead, Kat."

"And more will follow if we don't handle this correctly." Katrina's voice hardened. "This station represents not just billions in investment, but research that could change everything we know about energy, and the possibilities are limitless. If people find out two died up here in an accident, they'll protest to get us shut down, especially after Novus. Why do you think we are up here in the first place?"

"Maybe they should," Cira shot back. "If our security protocols can be breached that easily—"

Cira wanted to argue further, but exhaustion was pulling at her. And beneath the anger, a nagging fear was growing. She'd been exposed to deorum energy—an unstable form that had never been properly studied. What did that mean for her? For this impossible child?

"What about my exposure?" she asked. "The radiation—"

"Dr. Brown has run every test available. You appear to be unaffected, but we'll continue monitoring." Katrina's expression softened a touch. "I'm not unsympathetic, Cira. I know you were trying to prevent this. But what's done is done—and now we need to protect our research, the station, and everyone on it."

Before Cira could respond, the door slid open and Dalen rushed in, ignoring Dr. Brown's protests behind him. His face was bruised on one side, a bandage covering his left forearm, but he was moving under his own power.

"Cira." The relief in his voice was evident. He stopped short when he noticed Katrina. "Director. I didn't realise you were here."

"I was just leaving." Katrina nodded to them both. "Remember what we discussed, Cira."

After she left, Dalen moved to Cira's bedside, taking her hand in his. "You scared the hell out of me."

Cira stared at him, still reeling from Katrina's revelation. Should she tell him? How could she explain something she didn't understand herself?

"I'm okay." She tried to smile, but it felt forced. "You?"

"Knocked around a bit when the monitoring bay ceiling partially collapsed. Nothing serious." His expression darkened. "It's a mess out there. Processing level two is obliterated. They're saying it'll take months to rebuild."

"And Mills? Santos?" She had to ask, though she already knew the answer.

Dalen's grip on her hand tightened. "They didn't make it. I'm sorry."

They sat in silence for a moment, the weight of loss settling between them. Finally, Dalen spoke again, his voice lower.

"Something's not right about all this. The way they're handling it... Kat's got security confiscating personal devices, restricting comm access. It's like they're more worried about information getting out than figuring out what happened."

"She thinks it was sabotage. Someone wanted the ore to destabilise."

Dalen's expression hardened. "She's right. I saw the system logs. Someone knew exactly what they were doing—and they had high-level access codes to do it."

Before they could discuss it further, Dr. Brown returned, firmly insisting that Cira needed rest. Dalen squeezed her hand one last time before leaving, promising to return later.

When the door closed, Cira waited only moments before managing to push herself upright. The room tilted, then steadied. She yanked the monitoring patch from her wrist, silencing the alarm before it could sound, and made her way to the medical console near the wall. Her legs trembled beneath her, muscles weak from disuse.

She pressed her palm against the scanner, relieved when it recognised her clearance. The display flickered to life, bathing her face in blue light. Three keystrokes and she found her file—saw the blood work, the hormone levels, the genetic markers. The numbers didn't lie. Impossible as it was, the evidence was there in cold, clinical data.

Pregnant. Six weeks, according to the estimate.

As a scientist, she'd spent her career in pursuit of empirical truth. Now the truth was staring back at her from the screen, and she had no framework to process it. This wasn't just unexpected—it was biologically impossible. She'd seen her own medical records from Sacramentum. There was no mistaking what the doctors had told her.

Cira stared at the screen, her mind racing backwards through time. Six weeks ago? She and Dalen had been working opposite shifts, without ever crossing paths in their quarters. The Praetorium inspection had consumed her days while he handled the night cycle monitoring. They'd been like ghosts in each other's lives.

"That can't be right," she asked herself, fingers trembling over the console.

The last time they'd been intimate was during the station's maintenance shutdown—nearly three months ago. She remembered because it had been rare to have an entire day off together, a luxury they'd savoured.

Six weeks ago, she'd been alone, exhausted, falling asleep over research notes. No passionate encounters, no failed contraception. Nothing that could explain this.

Unless...

A memory surfaced: that strange power surge in the lab when she'd been working late. The momentary shimmer in the air, like reality itself had hiccupped. She'd dismissed it as fatigue, but what if something had happened? What if the ore had done something to her even then?

"What are you?" she said as her hand drifted to her abdomen. Fear and wonder tangled in her chest as she contemplated the impossible life growing within her—a child conceived without conception.

The room suddenly felt too small, the air too thin. She stumbled back to the bed, collapsing onto its edge. Exhaustion washed over her in waves, pulling her down into darkness.

And in that darkness, something waited.

She closed her eyes, surrendering to it. The medical bay dissolved around her, replaced by a vast expanse of stars. But these weren't the stars she knew—they pulsed with awareness, with intention. Time flowed differently here, stretching and compressing like a living thing. She felt herself fragmenting, consciousness splintering into countless versions of herself, each experiencing a different moment in time. In one, she held a child with eyes that reflected starlight. In another, she stood before a great machine, its heart pulsing with familiar golden light. In yet another, she knelt in ruins, blood on her hands.

Divided shall be made whole.

The voice echoed through her, resonating at a frequency that made her bones vibrate. It wasn't speaking to her—it was speaking *through* her, using her as a conduit for something vast and incomprehensible.

The child is the bridge.

She gasped, eyes flying open, reality crashing back with brutal force. The steady beep of monitors, the soft hum of the station's air recyclers—all of it seemed sharper, more present than before. She pressed a hand to her mouth, stifling a sob that threatened to tear free from her chest.

Whatever had happened to her in that containment breach—whatever was happening inside her now—it went beyond science, beyond reason.

For the first time in her life, Cira faced something she couldn't analyse or explain.

And it terrified her.

The quiet divide between before and after had been crossed, and there was no going back.

3

THE SHAPE OF WHAT'S COMING

The medical lab on Meridian's upper level had become Cira's home over the past six weeks. This small research space offered the privacy she increasingly valued as her condition became more unusual.

Cira adjusted the scanner over her abdomen, observing the data stream on her tablet. The embryo's development appeared normal by all conventional measures—size, neural tube formation, cardiac activity—yet the deorum particle concentrations surrounding it remained off the charts.

"You're going to damage that equipment if you keep recalibrating it."

Cira startled, looking up to find Katrina standing in the doorway. The Director moved into the lab with her characteristic quiet intensity, her eyes taking in the scattered equipment and data displays.

"I'm not getting accurate readings," Cira said, shutting down the scanner. "The deorum particles interfere with the imaging."

Katrina approached, studying the data on the nearest screen. "Have you experienced any new symptoms?"

Cira hesitated. The strange dreams—if they were dreams—had continued nightly. The sensations of disconnection from normal time. The moments when she'd reach for an object, only to find her hand passing through empty space where it should have been.

"Nothing significant," she said, knowing full well it wasn't true.

Katrina's eyes narrowed. "Dr. Brown reports you've been experiencing cognitive dissonance episodes. Perception distortions. Sensory anomalies."

"He shouldn't be sharing my medical information, even with you."

"He's concerned." Katrina pulled up a chair, sitting eye-level with Cira. It was an unusual gesture from someone who typically preferred to maintain the physical advantage of height. "As am I."

"I'm fine."

"You're changing," Katrina said, her professional tone softening into something more personal.

"And you're not?" Cira countered. "We haven't had a normal conversation since before the accident. When was the last time you asked about anything besides my symptoms? Your son asked about my daughter the other day, you know. He misses hanging out."

A look of pain crossed Katrina's face. "He doesn't understand why we can't visit you guys more often. I've tried to explain that work keeps us busy."

"The universal excuse," Cira said with a small smile. "I've used it myself."

"How is your daughter doing? Still tinkering with every electronic device she can find?"

"She sure is, caught her taking about a hand terminal last week." The brief moment of normacy felt like a lifeline. "She's worried about the new baby, though. Keeps asking if she'll have to share her room."

The lights stuttered, casting momentary shadows across the examination room. Cira grabbed the edge of the examination table, a wave of dizziness washing over her.

"Section 7 power relay," she said, eyes unfocused. "Junction box overheating. It's going to fail."

Katrina stared at her, alarm evident in her expression. "What did you just say?"

Before Cira could answer, her tablet chimed with an incoming alert. She glanced down at the screen, her face paling.

"System warning," she read aloud. "Thermal anomaly detected in Section 7 power relay. Maintenance crew dispatched."

The lights stuttered again, then stabilised.

"That's not possible," Katrina said, her voice barely audible. She moved to the lab's terminal so she could check the interface. "How did you know that?"

"I just... saw it." Cira pressed a hand to her temple, the dizziness receding. "Like it had already happened, but also hadn't yet. I can't explain it."

Katrina pulled up the station's maintenance logs, scrolling through recent reports. "This is the fourth documented incident. Last week, you predicted the atmospheric fluctuation in the hydroponics bay. Before that, the communications array malfunctioned."

"Those were educated guesses," Cira protested weakly. "I work with these systems every day."

"No one 'guesses' a specific junction box failure forty seconds before it happens." Katrina's expression hardened. "You're experiencing precognitive episodes, Cira. And they're becoming more frequent."

Cira's eyes darted past Katrina's shoulder, fixing on the observation window that offered a panoramic view of Meridian's barren surface. Her body went rigid, blood draining from her face.

"There's someone out there," she said, rising unsteadily to her feet.

"What?" Katrina turned to follow her gaze.

A man in a technician's uniform stood motionless on the rocky terrain, staring at the window. His form was clear against the rusty landscape—impossible given the lack of atmosphere, the crushing pressure, the deadly radiation bathing the surface.

"How is he breathing?" Cira moved toward the glass, drawn by a strange familiarity. "He's just... standing there."

The figure raised his hand in a slow, deliberate greeting. Recognition hit Cira—she knew him, somehow.

Katrina squinted, scanning the desolate vista. "Cira, there's nothing out there."

Cira turned to look at Katrina. "Right there!" Cira pressed her palm against the glass. "He's looking right at us!"

Katrina took Cira's arm, minding not to be too forceful, guiding her back to the examination table. "I don't see anyone. The surface is empty."

"But he's—" Cira turned back, and the figure had vanished as suddenly as he'd appeared.

"You need rest," Katrina said, her voice gentle but firm. "These episodes are taking a toll."

Cira felt cold dread settle in her stomach. She'd been trying to rationalise away the incidents, to find logical explanations for the impossible things happening to her. But hearing Katrina say it aloud made it real in a way she couldn't ignore.

"What's happening to me?" she asked.

Katrina closed the terminal window and turned to face her dead on. "The deorum exposure affected you differently than anyone else. Your proximity to the containment breach—it's created a unique situation."

"You mean I'm becoming something you can't predict or control?"

"I mean, you're experiencing neurological changes that we don't understand." Katrina leaned forward. "And if Praetorium finds out, they'll take you away from here. From your family."

The bluntness of the statement took Cira by surprise. "They wouldn't dare. I'm a senior researcher, not some lab specimen."

"Turner would, he'd do anything to advance his Electorum Project," Katrina said. "He runs Praetorium. What he says goes, for all eighty colonies. Since the Novus accident, his test subjects have been dwindling. He is desperate. If he learns that the ore potentially *created* a child inside you, a child that might be the ultimate temporal anomaly... He won't send doctors, Cira. He will send soldiers. You and your baby will become his personal experiment for the rest of your lives."

Cira stared at her, unable to speak. The Novus accident had been a catastrophic radiation leak that had forced the evacuation of the first settlement on Sacramentum. It was common knowledge. But test subjects? Special Projects? None of that had ever been mentioned in any official report.

"How do you know all this?" she asked.

Katrina's expression darkened. "Because I've seen his work firsthand. Before I came to Meridian, I was stationed at a research facility on Spes Ultima. What they did t here..." She shook her head. "It wasn't science. It was exploitation. And I won't let it happen to you or your child."

The terminal chimed, displaying an incoming message. Katrina glanced at it, her posture stiffening.

"Shit. The Praetorium team arrives tomorrow. Earlier than expected." She turned back to Cira. "We need to be careful. Dr. Brown and I have created a cover story—pregnancy complications due to radiation exposure from the accident. It explains your regular medical visits without raising suspicion."

"And if they want to examine me themselves?"

"We'll deal with that if it happens." Katrina stood, moving toward the door. "In the meantime, document everything, but keep it secure. Trust no one from corporate. Not with this."

After Katrina left, Cira sat alone in the lab, not quite sure how to process the information she had just learned.

She placed both hands on her abdomen, trying to connect with the impossible life growing within.

"What are we becoming?" she said to the empty room.

For a moment—brief but unmistakable—she felt a response. Not a physical movement, but awareness that wasn't her own. A consciousness that shouldn't yet exist, reaching back to her across the boundaries of time and development.

And in that moment, Cira understood that whatever was happening to her, whatever she was becoming, she wasn't facing it alone.

* * *

Dr. Brown's office was the smallest on Meridian, a converted storage closet that almost didn't fit his desk and two chairs. What it lacked in space, it made up for in privacy—the one commodity Katrina valued above all others tonight.

"You can't be serious." Brown stared at her across his cluttered desk, the holographic readouts of Cira's latest scans casting a blue glow between them. "This is a Class One reportable anomaly. Praetorium protocols are explicit."

Katrina leaned forward, keeping her voice low despite the room's sound-dampening. "And what do you think will happen when Praetorium learns we have a pregnant woman exhibiting kinetic displacement symptoms?"

"They'll provide resources. Specialists. This is beyond our capabilities."

"Their specialists won't come to treat her, John." Katrina rarely used his first name. "They'll come to study her. And when they're done, neither she nor her child will ever see Sacramentum again."

Brown removed his glasses, pinching the bridge of his nose. The gesture aged him, revealing the strain he was under "You don't know that."

"I do." Katrina tapped a command into her tablet, bringing up a classified document. She turned it toward Brown. "Turner has been explicit about needing more subjects displaying these kinds of signs since the Novus accident. If he thinks for a second we have a woman who is pregnant because of deorum ore, he's going to take her away, and she'll never see more than the inside of a laboratory. She already has a daughter. I just want them to be a family, not part of his Project."

Brown read the document, his expression darkening. "This doesn't specify human subjects."

"It doesn't exclude them either." Katrina took back the tablet. "And you know as well as I do how Praetorium operates."

"What is the project this is referring to?"

"Nothing you need concern yourself with." Katrina stood, pacing the small confines of the office. "What matters is protecting Cira and her child until we understand what's happening."

Brown shook his head. "You're making a dangerous calculation, Director. If Praetorium discovers we withheld information—"

"They won't discover anything if we're careful." She turned to face him. "This team arriving tomorrow is just a routine inspection. We've already had the initial assessment six weeks ago. This is bureaucratic box-checking. They have no specific reason to examine Cira."

"Unless someone tells them to look." Brown's eyes narrowed. "The accident wasn't just an accident, was it? That's what this is actually about."

Katrina's expression remained neutral, but her silence spoke volumes.

"My God." Brown leaned back in his chair. "You think someone deliberately caused the containment breach."

"I know they did." Katrina's voice hardened. "The refinement parameters were modified using high-level access codes. Someone wanted that ore to destabilise."

"But why?"

"I have theories." She returned to her seat. "None of which matters right now. What matters is that whoever caused this may have an agent on Meridian. And if they learn about Cira's condition—"

"They might consider her a specimen to extract to study." Brown finished the thought, his face paling. "Or worse, an unexpected variable to be eliminated."

"Exactly." Katrina nodded. "So we keep this contained. You, me, and Cira. No one else knows the full extent of her condition."

"What about her husband? Dalen should know what's happening to his wife."

Katrina hesitated. "Dalen is... impulsive. He acts first and considers consequences later. I'm not sure he'd handle this information with the discretion it requires."

"That's cold, even for you." Brown's disapproval was evident. "He deserves to know."

"What he deserves and what keeps his family safe may be different things." Katrina leaned into him. "I'm not taking any of this lightly, John."

"No, you never do." He sighed. "But I took an oath as a doctor. Withholding critical medical information from both my patient's family and my superiors violates everything I stand for."

"And if reporting it condemns them to becoming laboratory specimens?" Katrina challenged. "What does your oath say about that?"

Brown was silent for a long moment, studying the scans still hovering between them. Finally, he spoke. "Two weeks. I'll give you two weeks to gather more data to build a case for keeping her here under our supervision. After that, I make my own decision about reporting."

"Fine. Two weeks." Katrina stood. "In the meantime, I need you to create a medical cover story. Something plausible to explain her regular visits to your lab without raising suspicion."

"Pregnancy complications due to radiation exposure." Brown nodded. "Common enough after an accident like this, and it would justify the additional monitoring."

"Good." Katrina moved to the door, then paused. "Her precognitive abilities—they're accelerating. Keep tracking them. If she starts showing more pronounced displacement, I want to know right away."

"You believe it could go that far?"

"I think we're in uncharted territory." Katrina's expression was grim. "And I think we need to be prepared for anything."

Brown nodded. "I'll keep you updated. Daily reports."

"Make it twice daily." Katrina opened the door. "And John, thank you."

The doctor looked surprised at the rare show of gratitude. "For what?"

"For caring about her as a person, not just a patient." She stepped into the corridor. "That's rarer than it should be these days."

Katrina stepped into the corridor, her mind already thinking through contingency plans. Three steps later, a shadow detached from an alcove. She reached for the stun baton in her coat pocket before recognising Dalen's lean frame.

"We need to talk." His voice was low, controlled, but she caught the underlying fear.

"Not here." She kept walking, expecting him to follow.

"I've seen the medical files." The words stopped her cold. "Brown's notes on Cira. All of them."

Katrina turned slowly, scanning the corridor. A security camera pivoted above them, its red eye blinking steadily. "Walk with me to the observation deck. The equipment malfunction needs assessment."

Dalen fell into step beside her, his head bowed, his breathing elevated. They passed two android technicians who nodded respectfully. Katrina smiled, maintaining the facade of routine administration.

"How did you access secured medical files?" she asked once they were alone in the lift.

"Decryption algorithm." Dalen's expression remained neutral. "I wrote it myself. Brown's too trusting, it's my job to maintain the systems on this station, no one knows them like me."

The lift doors opened to the observation deck—a panoramic view of Sacramentum's swirling atmosphere below them. Katrina moved to the environmental control panel and activated the atmospheric testing sequence. The soft hum of machinery would mask their conversation from any listening devices.

"Clever." She moved to the far corner, where the deck's curvature created a blind spot in the security coverage. "The cameras will show us discussing atmospheric readings."

Dalen followed, his eyes never leaving her face. "Is it true? The deorum displacement? The precognitive episodes?"

"Yes."

"And you weren't going to tell me?" His voice remained steady, but his hands clenched at his sides.

"I was protecting you both."

"By keeping me in the dark about my wife and unborn child?" A flash of anger broke through his composure. "That's not protection. That's control."

Katrina touched the control panel again, bringing up atmospheric readings as cover. "What are you planning to do with this information, Dalen?"

"Leave. Take Cira somewhere safe, away from Praetorium's reach." His eyes narrowed. "Unless you have a better suggestion?"

She studied him—the determination in his stance, the calculation behind his eyes. This wasn't just a worried husband; this was a man who'd already begun mapping escape routes.

"Where would you go? Every colony is under Praetorium jurisdiction. Your identities would likely be tagged in every system."

"We'd find a way."

"And when Cira's condition worsens? When does she need specialised care?"

Dalen's confidence faltered. "There must be somewhere."

Before Katrina could answer, another technician in a standard-issue jumpsuit rounded the corner, datapad in hand. He nodded curtly as he passed, eyes fixed on his screen.

Katrina stiffened, watching him until he disappeared down the corridor. "Do you know him? I don't recall seeing that face before."

Dalen didn't even glance in the technician's direction. "Don't change the subject. My wife is experiencing displacement from her own god damn reality, and you're worried about whether you've seen a fucking technician before or not. Our child might be affected. I need answers, not distractions." He used the control panel, bringing up a new set of atmospheric readings as cover.

"Listen, we need to focus. You're avoiding my question." His voice dropped lower. "If Meridian isn't safe and we can't go to another colony, what options does that leave us?"

"Dalen—" Katrina's eyes lingered on the corridor where the technician had disappeared. Something felt wrong about the encounter, but Dalen's intensity pulled her attention back.

"There are alternatives," she admitted. "But none without significant risk. We'd need to create a controlled environment where her condition could be monitored without Praetorium oversight."

"Then that's what we'll do." Dalen's determination hardened his features. "Whatever it takes."

Katrina lowered her voice further. "Look, I might have some contacts. Scientists who operate outside Praetorium oversight. People who helped me before..."

"Before what?"

"Before I came here." She waved away the question. "The point is, they might be able to help—but rushing into this would be catastrophic. Praetorium doesn't just let valuable assets walk away."

"My wife isn't an asset."

"Damn it, Dalen. To them, she is." Katrina's expression softened. "Give me time. Let me reach out to my contacts, see if I can establish a secure extraction plan. Meanwhile, act normal. Any deviation in your behaviour will trigger alerts."

Dalen looked out at the stars, weighing her words. "How long?"

"A few weeks. Maybe less."

"And I'm supposed to trust you'll actually help us?"

"No." Katrina met his gaze. "You're supposed to be smart enough to realise I want the same thing you do—to keep Praetorium from turning your family into laboratory specimens."

He studied her face, searching for deception. "If anything happens to them while I'm 'sitting tight'..."

"It won't." She turned back to the control panel. "Now, let's discuss these atmospheric readings before security wonders why we've been staring at the same data for ten minutes."

4

GLASS IN THE VEINS

Katrina watched through the observation window as the refined deorum ore glowed with a yellowish light.

"Containment holding at ninety-eight per cent," Cira said, her voice betraying no hint of the exhaustion Katrina knew she must feel. "Harmonic resonance stabilised."

Two weeks of non-stop work had led to this moment. Fourteen days of calculations, simulations, and meticulously controlled micro-extractions. Fourteen nights of minimal sleep and maximum risk.

"The molecular structure is maintaining coherence," Katrina confirmed, studying the readouts. "We've done it, Cira."

They had taken deorum ore—unstable, unpredictable, deadly—and transformed it into something new. Something controlled. Something usable. A crystal. A metal. The possibilities were now limitless.

"Deorium," Cira said. "That's what we should call it."

Katrina glanced at her colleague. In the light of the refinement chamber, Cira's face looked drawn, her cheekbones more prominent than they had been even a week ago. Her pregnancy, now almost four months along by normal standards, showed as a pronounced swell beneath her lab coat.

But it hadn't been four months. It had been nine weeks. The accelerated growth was just one of many concerning symptoms that Katrina had been monitoring.

"Deorium," Katrina said back, testing the word. "From the old Earth word for the gods?"

"Of the gods, Kat! Clearly, you never paid much attention in Latin classes. Seems fitting for something capable of what this stuff can do." Cira's hand moved unconsciously to her abdomen. "Besides, we need to call it something other than 'refined deorum ore' in the reports."

The reports. Katrina had a shiver creep up her spine. Praetorium had been demanding daily updates, applying increasing pressure for results. General Turner himself had sent three personal inquiries in the past week alone.

"Speaking of reports," Katrina said, "Dr. Brown has requested another session with you this afternoon."

Cira's expression hardened. "I don't have time. We need to run a full stability analysis on the Deorium."

"The analysis can wait an hour. Your health can't."

"My health is fine."

"Is it?" Katrina stepped closer, lowering her voice though they were alone in the monitoring bay. "You haven't slept more than three hours a night in two weeks. You're experiencing displacement episodes at increasing frequency. And yesterday, you moved a coffee mug across your desk without touching it."

Cira's eyes flashed with something—anger, fear, or perhaps both. "You're having me watched now?"

"I'm trying to protect you." Katrina sighed. "Brown is concerned, and rightfully so. If he files a report with Praetorium—"

"He wouldn't."

"He's a doctor first, Cira. And a Praetorium employee. He's already delayed longer than protocol allows."

A tense silence fell between them, broken only by the soft hum of equipment.

Cira nodded. "Fine. One hour with Brown. But then we finish the stability analysis."

"Thank you." Katrina turned back to the observation window, watching the Deorium crystal pulse with its newfound stability. "This is going to change everything, you know."

"It already has," Cira said, her hand still resting on her abdomen.

* * *

That night, Cira dreamed.

She floated in a sea of golden light. The void was a place she was now used to coming to; it crisscrossed with glowing filaments that stretched in all directions like a cosmic web. The small creatures moved along these strands with purpose, their fur capturing and amplifying the light.

They gathered around her, chittering in their language. One approached, its enormous eyes reflecting not just light now, but understanding. It placed its delicate paws against her consciousness, and images bloomed:

The Deorium pulsing in its chamber, sending invisible waves through the station.

A metal that is stronger than anything that has come before.

Her own body, translucent in the dream-light, veins and neural pathways illuminated with the same golden-blue energy.

The child within her, growing faster than nature intended, already aware, already reaching.

The creature moved its paws, and the strands of light around them shifted. Where they intersected, Cira saw brief glimpses of possibilities:

Herself in a white room, surrounded by equipment, faceless figures watching.

Her daughter crying, reaching for someone who wasn't there.

A woman with Kat's face, but older, sadder, working in a laboratory filled with golden light.

A girl with Cira's eyes and Dalen's smile, standing at a crossroads of light and shadow.

An android with an arm made of Deorium.

The creature touched her again, and understanding flowed between them:

The Deorium changes all it touches. Not randomly, but with purpose.

You are becoming its voice. It's hands. It's bridge.

The child is becoming its future.

As the vision began to fade, the creature made one final gesture—drawing its paws together, then slowly pulling them apart. Between them stretched a thin strand of golden light that didn't break, but instead grew stronger as the distance increased.

Then came the wordless understanding.

Connected across any distance.

Across time. Across worlds.

Remember.

Cira woke with tears on her face and the taste of metal in her mouth. In the darkness of her quarters, her hands glowed faintly golden for several seconds before fading back to normal.

She didn't need to check the time to know it was 3:17 AM. Just as she didn't need to wait for the medical scan to know that her pregnancy had advanced another week overnight.

The acceleration was increasing.

The next week passed in a blur of activity. The successful refinement of Deorium led to a flurry of tests, each confirming what they had initially suspected: they had created something revolutionary. The refined ore maintained all the energy signature of its raw form but with none of the instability. It could be safely handled, transported, and—most importantly—utilised in ways the raw ore never could be.

Katrina found herself working eighteen-hour days, split between the technical aspects of the research and the increasingly complex political manoeuvring required to keep Praetorium at bay. Every success with the Deorium brought more attention, more questions, and more demands.

And through it all, Cira's condition continued to progress in ways that defied medical explanation.

"Her cognitive processing speed has increased by thirty per cent," Dr. Brown reported during one of their private briefings. "Brain activity in regions associated with spatial awareness and pattern recognition is off the charts. And the telekinetic incidents are becoming more frequent."

"Can you control it?" Katrina asked, though she already suspected the answer.

"I can't even measure it, let alone control it." Brown's frustration was evident. "And the pregnancy... It's accelerating beyond anything I've ever seen. The fetus is developing at, near as damn it, twice the normal rate."

"Is the child healthy?"

"By all measurable standards, yes. Remarkably so." Brown shook his head. "But this isn't natural. We're in uncharted territory."

"Keep monitoring. Discreetly." Katrina rose to leave. "And Brown? The two-week deadline you gave me has passed."

The doctor met her gaze steadily. "I'm aware."

"And?"

"And I'm still gathering data." His expression was unreadable. "For now."

As Katrina left his office, she understood what he had meant by his comment, and she didn't like it one bit.

* * *

Meridian Station hummed with a new energy. The successful refinement of Deorium had transformed the mood from one of cautious recovery after the accident to one of scientific triumph. Even the regular crew members, who understood little of the technical details, sensed that something momentous had occurred.

Katrina found Cira in the main lab, surrounded by holographic models of molecules.

"The energy conversion ratio is holding steady at ninety-two per cent," Cira said without looking up. "We can increase output by another fifteen per cent before hitting diminishing returns."

"That's enough for today," Katrina said. "You need rest."

"I'm fine."

"You're not." Katrina stepped closer, lowering her voice. "Cira, look at me."

Cira raised her eyes. In the dim light of the lab, they seemed to glow faintly—a subtle golden sheen that hadn't been there before the accident.

"What do you see when you look at me?" Cira asked.

The question caught Katrina off guard. "I see my friend. My colleague. A brilliant scientist pushing herself too hard."

"Dr. Brown views me differently," Cira said. "He perceives an anomaly, an irregularity, something to analyse and document."

"He's concerned for your health."

"He's concerned for his career." Cira turned back to the holographic displays. "And you're concerned for yours. I understand. I'm a liability now."

"That's not true."

"Isn't it?" Cira waved a hand, and the molecular models rearranged themselves without her touching the controls. "I'm changing, Kat. Every day, I understand more. See more. The Deorium, the accident, my pregnancy—they're all connected in ways I'm only beginning to comprehend."

Katrina felt a chill run through her. "What do you mean?"

"The deorum ore wasn't just unstable that day. It was... reaching. Searching." Cira's eyes took on a distant look. "And it found me. Found us."

"Cira, you're not making sense."

"Not yet." A faint smile crossed Cira's face. "But I will. We all will."

5

All That We Leave Unsaid

Dr. Brown stared at the completed report on his screen, waiting to be sent. Twenty-three pages of medical data, observations, and analysis—all pointing to the inescapable conclusion that Cira was no longer fully human.

Or perhaps, he thought grimly, she was becoming more human than any of them had ever been.

The evidence was irrefutable. Accelerated neural development. Psychokinetic abilities. Precognitive episodes. A pregnancy advancing at nearly twice the normal rate, with fetal development that defied every medical textbook ever written.

And at the centre of it all, exposure to deorum ore—now refined into the substance they called Deorium.

Brown removed his glasses and rubbed his eyes. He'd delayed this report for as long as he could, stretching the boundaries of professional ethics and Praetorium protocol. Katrina had asked for two weeks. He'd given her three. But he couldn't justify further delay, not with Cira's condition advancing so rapidly.

His door chimed, and he minimised the report screen. "Enter."

Dalen stepped into the small office, his face set in lines of worry. "Doctor. Do you have a minute?"

Brown gestured to the chair across from his desk. "Of course. What can I do for you?"

"It's Cira." Dalen sat, leaning forward intently. "Something's happening to her, and no one will give me straight answers. Not her, not Katrina. I thought maybe you…"

"Medical confidentiality prevents me from discussing another patient's condition," Brown said.

"She's my wife." Dalen's voice rose. "And that's my child she's carrying. A child that shouldn't exist, according to every fertility specialist we've ever seen."

Brown remained silent, his ethical dilemma deepening by the second.

"Please," Dalen said. "I'm not asking for medical details. I just need to know if she's in danger. If they're in danger."

The desperation in the man's eyes was clear to see. Brown found himself weighing his professional obligations against basic human decency. Dalen deserved some form of truth, even if it couldn't be the whole truth.

"You know your wife experienced direct exposure to raw deorum energy during the accident," Brown said, making sure not to go into any sort of detail. "We're still assessing the long-term effects of that exposure."

"And the pregnancy? It's advancing too fast. Anyone can see that."

Brown nodded. "There appear to be acceleration effects, yes. But all indicators suggest the child is developing normally, just… faster."

"And Cira? Those headaches she tries to hide. The moments when she seems to... disappear mentally."

"I can't discuss specific symptoms." Brown held up a hand as Dalen began to protest. "But I can tell you that we're monitoring her condition. Director Wright has made it her personal priority."

Dalen studied him for a long moment. "You're planning to report this to Praetorium, aren't you? That's why everyone's walking on eggshells."

Brown's silence was answer enough.

"They'll take her away." Dalen's voice hardened. "You know that, right? Praetorium doesn't study people—they dissect them."

"I have a duty—"

"To your patient." Dalen stood abruptly. "Your duty is to my wife and my child. Not to some dictator six light years away."

"It's not that simple."

"It never is." Dalen moved toward the door, then paused. "Just remember that you're not just sending data. You're making a decision about my family's future. About whether my child grows up with both parents or becomes a laboratory specimen."

The door slid shut behind him, leaving Brown alone with his conscience and the minimised report still waiting on his screen.

He sat motionless for several minutes, weighing options, considering consequences. With a deep breath, he reopened the report and made a single, crucial edit.

Under "Recommended Action," he deleted the standard protocol calling for immediate transfer to Praetorium facilities. In its place, he wrote: "Subject requires continued observation in current environment. Relocation could destabilise the condition and compromise valuable research data."

It wasn't much—just a small buffer that might buy Cira a little more time. But it was the most he could do while still fulfilling his obligation to report.

With a heavy heart, Dr. Brown pressed transmit. The report disappeared from his screen, racing across secure channels to Praetorium—and eventually to General Turner.

"I'm sorry," he said, not that anyone was there to hear his apology.

That night, as Brown finally fell into troubled sleep, Cira floated once more in the golden void. But this time, she wasn't alone.

Brown was there—not his physical form, but his consciousness, represented by a pale red light that pulsed with confusion and fear.

"What is this?" his essence seemed to ask without words. "Where am I?"

Cira's awareness approached him gently. *You're dreaming, Doctor. But not just dreaming.*

Around them, the small creatures moved in cautious circles, their enormous eyes fixed on the newcomer. One broke from the group, approaching Brown's red light with deliberate steps.

"This isn't possible," Brown's consciousness protested. "This isn't real."

Reality is broader than you've been taught to believe, Cira communicated. *Watch.*

The creature reached out, touching Brown's essence with a delicate paw. Instantly, his red light flared brighter, and Cira could sense his shock as understanding flowed into him.

Images formed in the space between them:

The report he had sent, arriving at Praetorium, being read by cold eyes.

A team dispatched, not just to study Deorium, but to acquire Cira.

A laboratory deep within Praetorium's scientific complex, where other subjects—other anomalies—were already being studied.

A child born in captivity, never knowing freedom. Cira being discarded without the Anima flowing through her.

The creature withdrew its paw, and Brown's essence shook with the weight of what he had seen.

Now you understand, Cira's consciousness whispered to him. *Now you know what you've set in motion.*

Turner building an army, the electorum project in full motion.

"I didn't know," Brown's light fluctuated with regret. "I was following protocol. Doing my duty."

Some duties transcend protocol, Cira responded. *Some truths matter more than rules.*

The creatures moved again, forming a circle around them both. Their light intensified, creating a sphere that encompassed Cira and Brown. Within this sphere, new images appeared:

Brown destroying data. Hiding evidence.

Katrina and Brown working side by side to protect Cira.

A different path, a chance for escape.

The technician stood on the surface of the moon.

"I can't," Brown's essence gleamed with doubt. "They'll know. They'll find out."

Yes, Cira acknowledged. *Eventually, but by then, it might be too late for them. And just in time for us.*

As the vision began to fade and consciousness called them both back to the waking world, Cira left Brown with one final message:

Choose carefully, Doctor. Not all chains are visible. Not all prisons have walls.

Brown woke with a gasp, his heart pounding. The dream—if it was a dream—felt more real than his bedroom, more substantial than the sweat-soaked sheets tangled around him.

He reached for his tablet with shaking hands. The confirmation of his report's receipt glowed on the screen, along with a new message:

"Delegation departing within 24 hours. Prepare the subject for preliminary examination. Full documentation required."

Brown stared at the words, the dream-vision of Cira in a Praetorium laboratory still burning in his mind.

What had he done?

And more importantly, what would he do now?

* * *

Three weeks after Brown filed his report, Cira stood before the refinement chamber, watching the Deorium with its now-familiar golden-blue light. Her reflection in the reinforced glass showed a woman transformed—not just by pregnancy, now you could see she was advanced beyond her actual term, but by something deeper.

Her eyes caught the light differently now, reflecting golden highlights that hadn't been there before. Her movements had acquired a fluidity, as if she operated just ahead of time itself. And around her, small objects would sometimes shift position when her concentration lapsed—pens rolling across desks, coffee cups sliding closer to her hand.

The door to the lab slid open, and Katrina entered. One look at her face told Cira everything she needed to know.

"They're coming, aren't they?" Cira asked without turning from the Deorium.

"A delegation from Praetorium." Katrina moved to stand beside her. "Arriving in three days."

"Led by Turner himself?"

"No. But close enough. His chief scientific advisor and a security detail."

Cira nodded, unsurprised. "Brown's report reached the right eyes then."

"He tried to protect you," Katrina said. "Added a recommendation against relocation. But the data itself was... compelling."

"I don't blame him." Cira placed a hand on her abdomen, now large enough to suggest a pregnancy of six months rather than the twelve weeks it had actually been. "He did what he thought was right."

"We could hide you." Katrina's voice dropped to a whisper. "There are places on Sacramentum where Praetorium has no reach. The old mining tunnels, the abandoned sections of Novus—"

"And turn my family into fugitives?" Cira shook her head. "I want my children to have stability, not a life on the run."

"I did some digging around," Katrina said, her voice even lower. "About contacts off-world. People outside the colonies who might help. People who operate beyond Praetorium's reach."

"No one is outside Turner's reach." Cira gave a short, bitter laugh. "There's nothing beyond the colonies except empty space and death."

"They'll take you to Praetorium. You and the baby."

"Perhaps." A faint smile crossed Cira's face. "Or perhaps not. The future isn't as fixed as it once was, at least not to me."

Katrina studied her. "What do you see, Cira? When you look ahead, what do you see?"

"Possibilities. Branching paths. Some clearer than others." Cira turned from the Deorium to face Katrina. "In some, yes, they take us to Praetorium. In others... different outcomes emerge."

"Can you control which path we take?"

"I'm learning to." Cira gestured toward a nearby tablet, which slid across the table toward her hand without being touched. "Just as I'm learning to try and control this."

Katrina's expression darkened with concern. "These abilities—the strain on your system—"

"Is necessary." Cira's voice took on an edge. "What's happening to me isn't random, Kat. Its purposeful. The Deorium, the pregnancy, the changes—they're all connected."

"Connected how?"

"I don't fully understand yet." Cira looked back at the refinement chamber. "But I know the deorum that flows through this planet is more than just an energy source. It's... aware, in its way. And it's preparing us for something."

"Us?"

"Humanity." Cira's hand moved to her belly again. "Starting with this child."

Katrina shook her head, alarm evident in her expression. "Cira, listen to yourself. You're attributing consciousness to a mineral. This isn't science—it's mysticism."

"Is it?" Cira's eyes flashed golden in the chamber's light. "Or is it just science we don't yet understand? The line between the two has always been thinner than we pretend."

"This isn't you talking," Katrina said. "This is the deorum exposure affecting your cognition."

"Or expanding it." Cira stepped closer. "You've seen the data, Kat. My neural pathways aren't degrading—they're reorganising. Forming new connections. Accessing parts of the brain we don't understand."

"At what cost? Your body is under enormous strain. The accelerated pregnancy alone—"

"Is proceeding exactly as it should." Cira's voice softened. "The child is healthy, Kat. Perfect in every way. Just... arriving sooner than expected."

"Brown can't even determine the sex," Katrina said. "The scans show... interference. Distortion around the fetus that makes detailed imaging impossible."

"Perhaps some things aren't meant to be known in advance."

Katrina fell silent, studying her friend with a mixture of concern and scientific fascination. Finally, she asked the question that had been haunting her for weeks.

"What is this child, Cira? What will it be?"

"Hope." Cira's answer came without hesitation. "A bridge between what we are and what we could become."

Before Katrina could respond, the lab's communication system chimed with an incoming message. She moved to the console and read the alert, her expression growing grave.

"What is it?" Cira asked.

"The delegation from Praetorium." Katrina looked up, her face pale. "They've moved up their arrival. They'll be here tomorrow."

Cira nodded calmly. "Then we have work to do."

"What kind of work?"

"Preparation." Cira turned back to the Deorium, watching its pulsing light with determination. "They're coming for the Deorium and for me. But they'll find more than they bargained for."

"Cira—"

"Trust me, Kat." Cira's eyes met hers, and for a moment, the golden glow seemed to intensify. "The paths are converging now. And not all of them lead to Praetorium."

Inside, despite her outward confidence, Cira felt a flutter of doubt. The visions that came to her now showed multiple futures, yes—but in how many of them did she remain free? In how many did her child grow up safe from those who would study and exploit it?

Too few, she admitted silently. Far too few.

But she would fight for those few possibilities with everything she was becoming. For her family. For the child growing within her who would change everything.

6

THE WEIGHT OF KNOWING

The Praetorium shuttle docked with Meridian Station on schedule. No fanfare, no ceremony—just the metallic thunk of docking clamps engaging and the soft hiss of pressure equalisation.

Katrina stood at the airlock, back straight, face composed into a mask of professional courtesy. Beside her, Dr. Brown fidgeted with the cuff of his uniform, his usual clinical detachment betrayed by the sheen of sweat on his forehead.

"Remember," Katrina said, "stick to the official report. Nothing more."

Brown gave a firm nod as the airlock cycled open.

Four figures emerged. First came a woman with close-cropped silver hair and the rigid posture of military command, though she wore the charcoal grey uniform of Praetorium's scientific division. Behind her, two security officers—expressionless and armed—flanked a slender man, who was taking in every detail of the docking bay.

"Director Wright." The fiery red-headed woman extended a hand. "Dr. Emilia Voss, Chief Scientific Advisor to

General Turner. Thank you for accommodating our accelerated schedule."

"Dr. Voss." Katrina shook the offered hand, noting its cool firmness. "Welcome to Meridian. This is Dr. Brown, our Chief Medical Officer."

Voss nodded to Brown, then gestured to the pale-eyed man. "This is Dr. Reyes, our physics specialist. And Lieutenants Ashcraft and Okoniewski, security."

No hands were offered by the others. Reyes gave a slight nod, while the security officers remained impassive, their eyes constantly scanning the docking bay.

"I trust your journey was comfortable," Katrina said, falling back on diplomatic pleasantries.

"It was efficient," Voss said. "As I hope our work here will be. We'd like to begin right away."

"Of course. I've prepared the main conference room for your briefing, and—"

"That won't be necessary." Voss cut her off with a thin smile. "We'll need direct access to your refinement facilities and the subject."

"Subject?" Katrina kept her expression neutral.

"Cira." Voss's eyes hardened. "Let's not waste time with pretences, Director Wright. We've read Dr. Brown's report thoroughly. We know what's happening here, as do you."

Brown shifted uncomfortably beside Katrina. "My report recommended continued observation in her current environment. Any disruption could—"

"Your recommendations have been noted, Doctor." Voss's tone made it clear how little those recommendations mattered. "Now, shall we proceed? Time is a factor."

As they moved from the docking bay into the station proper, Lieutenant Ashcraft spoke quietly into his comm unit. Throughout Meridian, security protocols activated in response—door locks engaging, surveillance systems coming online, communications channels being rerouted through Praetorium filters.

The station was being locked down, one system at a time, and staff would be rotated off the station, just leaving the android technicians to man the systems.

Katrina noticed, of course. It was her station. But she said nothing, leading the delegation toward the labs with a deliberate pace that betrayed none of her growing alarm.

"I should mention," she said, "that Cira's condition requires careful handling. The deorum exposure has made her... sensitive to certain stimuli."

"We're well aware of the potential complications," Dr. Reyes spoke for the first time, his voice surprisingly deep for his slight frame. "That's why we're here."

They reached the main laboratory level, where Cira waited. Katrina had insisted she remain in the primary lab rather than the refinement chamber, keeping her separated from the Deorium, seemed prudent given the circumstances.

The door slid open to reveal Cira sitting calmly at a workstation, reviewing data on a holographic display. She looked up as they entered, her golden-flecked eyes taking in the delegation with unsettling serenity.

"Good morning, Dr. Langley." Voss stepped forward. "I'm Dr. Emilia Voss. We are from Praetorium. These are my colleagues. We're here to assist with your... unique situation."

Cira's gaze moved from face to face, lingering on the security officers before returning to Voss. "No, you're not," she said.

A brief silence followed, broken by Voss's nervous laugh. "I beg your pardon?"

"You're not here to assist me." Cira's voice remained calm, matter-of-fact. "You're here to determine if I'm a threat or an asset. And then to contain me accordingly."

Reyes stepped forward, interest sharpening his pale eyes. "Fascinating. The perception enhancement is even more advanced than the report suggested."

"It's not perception." Cira turned her attention to him. "It's pattern recognition. The same patterns have played out across history whenever something new and powerful emerges. First comes fear, then control, then exploitation."

"Cira" Voss's voice hardened, "I assure you, Praetorium has only the best interests of—"

"Please don't lie." Cira cut her off. "It wastes time, and as you said to Director Wright in the docking bay, time is a factor."

Voss's eyes narrowed at the reference to a conversation Cira couldn't possibly have heard. She glanced at the security officers, who subtly shifted their positions, hands moving closer to their weapons.

Katrina stepped forward, placing herself between Cira and the delegation. "Cira is still adjusting to the neurological changes caused by the exposure. Perhaps we should begin with a review of the Deorium refinement process instead."

"An excellent suggestion." Voss nodded, though her eyes remained fixed on Cira. "Dr. Reyes will stay here to conduct a preliminary assessment. The rest of us will review the refinement chamber."

It wasn't a request. Katrina hesitated, reluctant to leave Cira alone with any of them, but a subtle nod from her friend gave her permission.

"This way, then," Katrina said, leading Voss and one of the security officers toward the door. Dr. Brown moved to follow, but Voss stopped him.

"Dr. Brown, you'll remain here with Dr. Reyes. Your medical insights will be valuable during the initial assessment."

Brown glanced uncertainly at Katrina, who gave him a reassuring nod before departing with Voss and Lieutenant Ashcraft. Lieutenant Okoniewski remained at the laboratory door, her posture relaxed but vigilant.

As the door closed behind them, Reyes turned to Cira with undisguised fascination.

"Now then, Cira", he said, pulling up a chair to sit across from her. "Why don't we discuss what you're becoming?"

* * *

By evening, Meridian Station had been thoroughly transformed. What had been a collaborative scientific outpost was now effectively a Praetorium detention facility. Additional security personnel had arrived on a shuttle from Sacramentum, establishing checkpoints at key junctions throughout the station. All communications were monitored, all movements tracked.

Katrina sat alone in her office, staring at the secure tablet Voss had left with her. On it, a classified file detailed the "Deorum Anomaly Containment Protocols" that would be implemented starting tomorrow. The clinical language couldn't disguise the truth: Cira would be sedated, placed in a specialised containment unit, and transported to Praetorium's main research facility.

The child she carried would be monitored continuously. Upon delivery—natural or induced—it would be transferred to a separate research division.

They would never see each other again.

Katrina closed the file, feeling physically ill. She had known Praetorium would take control, but the cold efficiency of their plans exceeded even her worst expectations.

Her comm unit chimed with an incoming message. Restricted channel, no identification code. Under normal circumstances, she would have reported such an anomaly without hesitation. But these were not normal circumstances.

She accepted the transmission.

No video appeared, only a text message, encrypted with a cypher she recognised from her early days working with Praetorium intelligence:

K—

Options exist beyond what appears possible.

Turner offers terms: Your expertise for their safety.

The Black division requires your specific knowledge again.

Alternative: Containment protocol extends to all involved.

**A decision is required before transport.
Coordinates and authentication follow.
—M**

Katrina stared at the message, her blood running cold. The meaning was clear beneath the sparse wording. General Turner was offering her a position back in the Black Division—Praetorium's most secretive research group—in exchange for Cira and her child's safety. If she refused, the "containment protocol" would extend to everyone with knowledge of Cira's condition.

Including her. Including Brown. Including Dalen and their daughter. Including her own husband and her son.

The alternative was unthinkable.

She had spent so long getting out of that life, away from what happened, she should've known you can never truly get away, they just let you on a longer leash till they need you again.

Before she could ponder further, a second message appeared:

Verification: Sacramentum-Echo-7-9-3

To accept: Leave on transport tomorrow.

To refuse: Do nothing.

You know what happens to anomalies that Praetorium cannot control.

The verification code was one she hadn't seen in years—from a classified project she'd worked on before coming to Meridian. Only a handful of people would know to use it. After what happened at Spes Ultima, they promised her she could choose her own directives.

Katrina deleted both messages, then wiped the comm unit's buffer. Her mind raced through possibilities, each more desperate than the last. If she accepted this offer, she would be separated from her own family, potentially forever. If she refused... she wouldn't have a family left to be separated from.

A soft knock at her door interrupted her thoughts. "Enter," she called, composing her features.

Dr. Brown stepped inside, looking haggard. The day's "assessments" had taken their toll on him.

"They've sedated her," he said without preamble. "Against my medical recommendation."

"Voss?"

"Reyes." Brown sank into a chair. "He claimed she was becoming agitated, but that's not true. She was perfectly calm. Too calm, actually, given what they were doing."

"What were they doing?" Katrina asked, though she feared she already knew.

"Invasive neural scans. Tissue sampling. They're treating her like a laboratory specimen, not a patient." Brown's voice cracked. "I tried to intervene, but..."

"But you were reminded of your place in the hierarchy," Katrina finished for him.

He nodded miserably. "I did this. My report—"

"You did what you thought was right, John," she said, more harshly than intended. "As we all did. And now we're seeing the consequences."

Brown studied her face. "You have a plan, don't you? Something you're not telling me."

Katrina considered her options. Brown was a good man, a good doctor. But he had already proven he would follow Praetorium's rules when pressed. Could she trust him with this?

"No plan," she lied. "Just regrets."

He didn't look convinced, but nodded anyway. "They're transporting her tomorrow. 0800 hours. A shuttle is being equipped with a containment unit as we speak."

"And the Deorium?"

"Being prepared for transport as well. Reyes is personally overseeing the containment procedures."

"God damn it, that's my research," Katrina nodded, her decision crystallising. "Get some rest, Doctor. Tomorrow will be... difficult."

After Brown left, Katrina sat motionless for several minutes, weighing the cost of what she was about to do. She activated her personal hand terminal—one not connected to Meridian's main systems—and began composing a message to her husband on Sacramentum.

It would be the hardest letter she had ever written.

* * *

The transport preparations began at 0600, two hours before the scheduled departure. Meridian Station hummed with tense activity as Praetorium personnel secured their precious cargo—both the Deorium samples and Cira.

Katrina watched from the observation deck as technicians in protective gear transferred sealed containers of refined Deorium into specialised transport units. Each container was monitored for the slightest fluctuation in energy signature.

"Impressive operation," Dr. Voss said, appearing beside her. "Efficiency has always been Praetorium's strength."

"Among other things," Katrina said neutrally.

Voss studied her profile. "You disapprove of our methods, Director."

"I disapprove of treating a pregnant woman like a dangerous specimen."

"But that's exactly what she is." Voss's voice remained clinical, devoid of malice but equally devoid of compassion. "Cira's transformation presents both extraordinary potential and extraordinary risk. Surely you can see that."

"I see a friend being taken from her family."

"A necessary precaution." Voss turned back to the activity below. "The anomalies she's exhibiting are unprecedented. The telekinetic capabilities alone would classify her as a security risk, even without the accelerated pregnancy and cognitive enhancements."

Katrina said nothing, watching as another container of Deorium was sealed and logged.

"You've received an offer," Voss said after a moment, her voice lower. "Have you considered it?"

So Voss knew about the message. Katrina kept her expression neutral. "I've considered many things in the past twelve hours."

"Black Division, they need you back. Your expertise with metaphysics makes you uniquely qualified."

"And my friendship with Cira makes me uniquely motivated," Katrina added.

Voss actually smiled. "In my experience, the best scientists are those with personal investment in the outcome."

"And what outcome does Turner envision?"

"Control," Voss said. "Of the most powerful force humanity has ever encountered."

"Why now? Why does he need the Deorium?"

"To connect the network of gates." Voss turned to face her. "The Deorium is merely a conduit. What flows through it—that's the true prize."

A commotion below drew their attention. One of the Deorium containers was showing energy fluctuations, its monitoring systems flashing warning signals. Technicians moved with controlled urgency to stabilise it.

"Even refined, it remains unpredictable," Voss said. "Much like your friend."

"Perhaps that's the point," Katrina said. "Some things aren't meant to be controlled."

Voss's comm unit chimed. She checked it, then straightened. "They're ready to move Cira to the shuttle. Your presence is requested."

"Why?"

"She's asking for you." A hint of irritation crossed Voss's face. "Despite the sedation, she's been remarkably... insistent."

Katrina followed Voss to the medical bay, where Cira had been kept overnight. The room was crowded with medical personnel and security officers, all focused on the containment stretcher in the centre.

Cira lay strapped to it, an array of monitoring devices attached to her body. Her eyes were half-open, glazed from the sedatives but still tracking movement. Her pregnancy was unmistakable now, her abdomen swollen far beyond what twelve weeks should show.

When she saw Katrina, she struggled weakly against the restraints. "Kat," she said, her voice slurred but urgent.

Katrina moved to her side, taking her hand. "I'm here."

"They can't control it," Cira said. "None of us can. Remember that."

"Save your strength," Katrina said, aware of Voss watching her.

"My daughter, on the surface," Cira said, her grip tightening with surprising strength. "Promise me..."

"I'll make sure she's taken care of," Katrina assured her, fighting to keep her voice steady. "Dalen too."

Cira's eyes cleared momentarily, the golden flecks brightening. "You know what's coming. I've shown you."

Had she? Katrina couldn't remember any such conversation, but something in Cira's intensity made her nod anyway.

"It's time," Voss said. "We need to move her now to maintain our departure schedule."

Cira's grip tightened again. "Choose wisely," she said, so low that only Katrina could hear. "Not all chains are visible. Not all prisons have walls."

The words sent a chill through Katrina—they echoed the dream Cira had the night before, a dream of golden light and impossible choices.

"Sedate her again," Voss asked one of the medical technicians. "We can't risk any incidents during transport."

"Wait," Katrina said, an idea forming. "Let me speak with her privately for a moment. She'll be more cooperative if I explain what's happening."

Voss hesitated, then nodded. "Two minutes. Everyone else out."

The room cleared, leaving Katrina alone with Cira. As soon as the door closed, Cira's eyes sharpened, the drugged haze receding.

"How are you fighting the sedative?" Katrina asked, amazed.

"The deorum changed me," Cira said, her voice stronger than it had been moments ago. "Listen. We don't have much time."

"I received an offer from Turner," Katrina said. "To join the Black Division."

"I know." Cira nodded. "You have to accept it."

"If I do, I'll never see my family again. My husband, my son—"

"If you don't, none of us has a future." Cira's eyes locked with hers. "This isn't just about me, or my child, or even the Deorium. There's something bigger happening, Kat. Something I can't explain yet. But you need to be at Praetorium when it does."

"How can you know that?"

"The same way I know you've been planning your own death since last night." Katrina raised her hand to her mouth as she took a step back. "It's the right choice. The only choice that creates a path forward."

Before Katrina could respond, the door slid open and Voss re-entered with the medical team.

"Time's up," she said. "Let's move."

As they wheeled Cira toward the shuttle bay, Katrina fell into step beside Dr. Brown, who looked as though he hadn't slept at all.

"This is wrong," he said under his breath. "All of it."

"Yes," Katrina agreed. "It is."

The procession reached the shuttle bay, where the final preparations were underway. The Deorium containers had already been loaded and secured in a specialised hold at the rear of the craft. Now the medical team moved Cira's stretcher up the loading ramp, careful to keep the monitoring equipment stable.

Dr. Reyes supervised the loading personally, his pale eyes constantly darting between Cira and the readouts from her monitors. "Fascinating," he said as one of the screens showed an unusual neural pattern. "Even sedated, the activity continues."

"Director Wright," Voss called, gesturing Katrina over. "A moment before we depart."

Katrina approached, her face composed.

"Your decision?" Voss asked.

Katrina glanced at the shuttle, where Cira was now being secured for the journey. Their eyes met briefly across the distance, and Katrina saw something there—not fear, but certainty. As if Cira could see the future unfolding before them all.

"I accept," Katrina said. "On one condition."

"You're hardly in a position to negotiate," Voss said, though her tone suggested otherwise.

"Cira and her child remain together. No separation. I want that guarantee in writing from Turner himself."

Voss considered this. "I'll convey your condition. But you understand what accepting means? You'll be declared dead in an unfortunate accident. Your family, your colleagues—none can know the truth."

"I understand." The weight of the decision pressed down on Katrina. *How can I vanish from existence? My son will never know what happened to me. Will he spend years searching, hoping?*

"When do we leave?"

"We've prepared a scenario. A shuttle malfunction during your return to Sacramentum tomorrow. No survivors, no recoverable remains." Voss's clinical detachment was almost admirable in its completeness. "You'll be on a different shuttle, of course. Bound for Praetorium."

"And Brown? The others who know about Cira's condition?"

"Will be contained in other ways." Voss's slight smile did nothing to soften the implied threat. "Less permanent, provided they cooperate."

The shuttle's engines began their pre-launch sequence, the low hum filling the bay. Final checks were being conducted, and the departure was only minutes away.

"I need to gather personal items," Katrina said. "Research notes."

"Already done." Voss nodded toward a small case near the second shuttle. "Everything deemed necessary has been collected. Anything else would compromise the cover story."

Of course. Praetorium's efficiency extended to every detail.

"Then I suppose there's nothing left to say," Katrina said.

"Just one thing." Voss stepped closer, her voice dropping. "When we arrive at Praetorium, you will be granted access to information that few ever see. The true nature of the Deorium. The larger project it serves. Once you know, there is no going back. Are you certain of your choice? The work you did at Spes Ultima hasn't been forgotten, you know?"

Katrina looked once more at the shuttle where Cira lay bound and sedated. Dr Brown, standing helplessly by as his patient was taken. At the station she had helped build, now under Praetorium's complete control.

Then she thought of her son. Of her husband, who would soon believe her dead. Of the message she had left for them, hidden where only he would think to look, explaining nothing yet asking for forgiveness.

"I'm certain," she said, the words burning her throat like acid.

Voss nodded, satisfied. "Then welcome to Black Division, Director. Your new life begins tomorrow."

And with that, the primary shuttle, that was due to carry Cira and the Deorium away from Meridian, powered down and the passengers unloaded again, Katrina watched with the hollow certainty that she had made a devil's bargain—one that would haunt her for the rest of her days.

But as Cira disappeared into the belly of the station, she remembered her words: "Not all chains are visible. Not all prisons have walls."

And not all sacrifices are in vain, she added silently, turning away from the emptying bay.

Tomorrow, Katrina, the Director of Meridian Station, would die.

And someone else—someone with access to secrets that might one day save—would be born.

7

BETWEEN THE SPARKS & SILENCE

The golden void pulsed with urgency, the strands of light surrounding Cira vibrating with tension. The small creatures moved along these pathways, their fur flashing with patterns she had learned to recognise as distress.

One approached, its enormous eyes reflecting not just light but images—parts of scenes playing out in rapid succession:

A shuttle departing Meridian.
Flames erupting from its engines.
Katrina's face, calm amid chaos.
A different shuttle, hidden from sensors, cutting through Sacramentum's atmosphere toward the stars.

The creature pressed its paws against Cira's consciousness, and understanding flooded through her:

Sacrifice necessary. Bridge protected.
Truth hidden within a lie.
Friend becomes guardian.
The path narrows. Choices dwindle.

The golden strands around them began to splinter, each fragment showing a different possibility:

Meridian breaking apart, atmosphere venting into space.

A baby crying, alone in darkness.

Dalen, face lined with determination, speaking to a shadowed figure.

A tiny hand reaching out, glowing with golden light.

The creatures gathered around her, moving in ways that seemed to stabilise the fracturing strands. Their message came not in words but in pure certainty:

Control slipping. Power growing.

Vessel strains to contain what it holds.

Seek the hidden path.

Trust what comes.

As the vision began to fade, one final image formed—Katrina standing in a sterile white laboratory, surrounded by containers of glowing Deorium, her face a mask of stern calculation as she worked on something the creatures deliberately obscured from Cira's sight.

Not dead. Transformed.

Remember.

* * *

Cira woke to alarms.

For a moment, she couldn't distinguish between the dream and reality—both filled with urgent warnings, both vibrating with tension. Then the station's emergency system cut through her confusion:

"All personnel report to emergency stations. Repeat, all personnel report to emergency stations."

She struggled to sit up, her advanced pregnancy making the movement awkward. The chronometer showed 0637—early morning. Too early for scheduled drills or maintenance.

Something was wrong.

The door to her quarters slid open, revealing Dalen's worried face. "You're awake. Good. We need to move to the secure area."

"What's happening?" Cira asked, knowing the answer would confirm her dream.

Dalen helped her to her feet, his movements gentle but urgent. "There's been an accident. Katrina's shuttle—" His voice caught. "It was returning to Sacramentum when something happened. They lost contact about twenty minutes ago."

The dream images flashed through Cira's mind: flames, Katrina's face, a hidden shuttle. "No," she said. "No, that's not what happened."

"They've dispatched search vessels, but—" Dalen stopped, studying her face. "What do you mean, that's not what happened?"

"She's not dead." The certainty of it hummed through Cira's veins. "She made a choice."

Dalen's expression shifted from concern to alarm. "Cira, you're not making sense. The shuttle exploded. There were no survivors."

"That's what they want everyone to believe." Cira moved toward the door, desperate to reach the command centre, to see the data for herself. "It's part of the plan."

"What plan? Whose plan?" Dalen caught her arm. "Cira, you need to calm down. The baby—"

"Is fine." She pulled away from him. "Better than fine. Connected. Aware. Like me."

The look on Dalen's face told her how she sounded—delusional, unstable. But she couldn't stop the words, couldn't contain the certainty flooding through her.

"Katrina made a deal," she said, moving into the corridor where other station personnel were hurrying toward their emergency stations. "With Praetorium. With Turner. She sacrificed herself to protect us."

"Cira, please." Dalen's voice took on an edge of desperation. "You're not well. The deorum exposure, the pregnancy—they're affecting your mind. Dr. Brown warned us this might happen."

"Brown doesn't understand what's happening. None of you do." She turned to face him, aware of others in the corridor stopping to stare. "I can see it, Dalen. All of it. The patterns, the connections, the paths forward and back."

"Ma'am," a security officer edged forward, hand hovering near his holstered stunner, "we need everyone to report to their designated safe areas until the situation is assessed."

"The situation," Cira said, her voice rising, "is that Katrina Wright isn't dead. She's gone to Praetorium as part of a deal to protect me and our child from being separated and experimented on. She faked her death to give herself freedom to work from within their system."

The security officer exchanged a worried glance with Dalen. "Sir, perhaps we should call Dr. Brown."

"No!" Cira stepped back, her back pressing against the cold corridor wall as the realisation struck her—a pregnant, wild-eyed woman with trembling hands and dishevelled hair— making wild claims about conspiracies and faked deaths. The rational part of her mind, still functioning beneath the flood of certainty, recognised the danger of her position.

If they sedated her, if they restricted her further, she would lose what little freedom remained. And without freedom, she couldn't protect her family from what was coming.

"I'm sorry," she said, forcing her voice to calm. "You're right. I'm... I'm not thinking clearly. The news about Kat is a shock."

Relief washed over Dalen's face. "Let's get you somewhere quiet. I'll stay with you."

She nodded, allowing him to guide her toward their quarters, away from the curious stares of the station personnel. But inside, the certainty remained undiminished. Katrina was alive. The dream had shown her the truth, just as it had shown her so many other truths in recent weeks.

The question was: what should she do with this knowledge?

And more importantly: what else had the dream been trying to tell her?

* * *

Three days after Katrina's 'death," Meridian Station settled into a hollow routine. The search had been called off after recovery vessels found debris consistent with catastrophic shuttle failure. Memorial services were held on both Meridian and Sacramentum, attended by solemn-faced officials who spoke of sacrifice and duty.

Cira attended neither. Instead, she remained in her quarters, refusing all visitors except Dalen and, now and again, Dr. Brown. The latter came with increasing frequency, his medical concern not even coming close to disguising his scientific fascination with her advancing condition.

"The accelerated development continues," he noted during one such visit, studying the scanner readouts. "Twenty-six weeks of fetal development in just over thirteen weeks of actual pregnancy. It's unprecedented."

"Is the baby healthy?" Cira asked the same question she always asked.

"By all measurable standards, yes." Brown's answer remained consistent as well. "Though the energy signature around the fetus makes detailed imaging difficult."

What he didn't say—what he didn't need to say—was that Praetorium would be keenly interested in these developments. With Katrina gone, Brown was now the highest-ranking scientist on Meridian, and his loyalties were being tested daily.

"Have you reported this to Praetorium?" she asked.

Brown's hesitation told her everything. "Protocol requires regular updates on all deorum research."

"That's not what I asked."

He sighed, setting down the scanner. "Yes. I've reported your condition. But I've also emphasised the risks of transport or separation. For now, they seem content to monitor from a distance."

"For now," Cira echoed bitterly. "Until the baby is born. Then what?"

Brown had no answer for that. They both knew what Praetorium wanted—the child, the mother, the Deorium. All under their direct control.

After he left, Cira sat alone in the dim light of her quarters, one hand resting on her swollen abdomen. The child within moved with increasing strength, each kick or turn accompanied by a faint golden glow visible beneath her skin in the darkened room.

"What are we going to do?" she asked the empty air.

As if in response, the environmental controls in her quarters fluctuated—lights brightening, then dimming, air circulation increasing, then stopping altogether for several seconds.

Cira sat up straighter, alarmed. Had she done that? The telekinetic incidents had been increasing, small objects moving when her emotions ran high, electronic systems sometimes seemed to be glitching in her presence. But nothing this significant.

Her comm unit chimed with an incoming message from station operations: "Dr. Langley, we're showing environmental fluctuations in your sector. Are you experiencing any issues?"

"Momentary power surge," she said. "Everything's stable now."

"Acknowledged. We'll send maintenance to check the systems."

"No need," she said. "I'm resting. I'd prefer not to be disturbed."

A pause. "Understood, Dr. Langley. Please report any further anomalies."

Cira closed the connection, her pulse hammering against her ribs. She needed to gain control of these abilities before they betrayed her. Before she endangered everyone on the station.

The door chimed, then slid open before she could respond. The door hissed open, revealing Dalen's silhouette framed in the corridor light, forehead creased with lines that hadn't been there yesterday.

"We need to talk," he said without preamble.

"About the environmental fluctuation? It was just a power surge—"

"About getting off Meridian." He sat beside her on the bed, voice dropping to a near-whisper. "All of us. Before Praetorium decides to take more direct action."

Cira stared at him. "What are you saying?"

"I'm saying Katrina was right." His eyes met hers, filled with a determination she hadn't seen in years. "There are people beyond Praetorium's reach. People who can help us disappear."

"No one is outside Turner's reach," she said, the same as she had the first time she heard it days ago, though with less conviction now.

"No, I spoke with her about it, I had to consider options early on, hun." Dalen leaned closer, "Real contacts. Real options. I've been making inquiries since... since the accident."

"How? All communications are monitored."

A small smile crossed his face. "Not all of them. Kat still had friends in places that Praetorium doesn't control. People who want to help."

Hope flickered in Cira's chest, quickly tempered by caution. "Even if such contacts exist, what could we possibly offer them? We have nothing of value."

"We have the most valuable substance in human space." Dalen's voice dropped even lower. "Deorium, and not just that, we have the plans of how to refine it."

Stealing Deorium from Praetorium would be considered high treason, punishable by execution. Even discussing it could be enough to condemn them.

"That's insane," she said. "The security around the refinement chamber—"

"I was able to access Kat's personnel files," Dalen said, his voice steady despite the risk in what he was confessing. "She had a hidden subroutine buried in the station's tertiary backup systems. It contained encrypted communication protocols—ones that bypass Praetorium's monitoring network."

Cira stared at him, disbelief warring with desperate hope. "How did you even find that?"

"Remember when I redesigned the station's emergency protocols after the security breach two years ago? I built in backdoors—just in case." His eyes darted to the door, then back to her. "Kat knew about them. She left breadcrumbs for someone like me to follow."

"And these contacts..." Cira rested a protective hand over her belly. "You trust them?"

"They're part of some sort of network. Former scientists, engineers—people who've seen what Praetorium does." Dalen took her hands in his, his knuckles turning white. "They can get us transport off Sacramentum. New identities, safe passage through the outer colonies."

The desperation in his voice was raw, unfiltered. This wasn't the calculated, cautious Dalen she knew. This was a man fighting for his family's survival.

"What about..." she said, thinking of their sixteen-year-old daughter on the surface.

"I've already contacted Grace. She'll go to our apartment on Sacramentum and get her. They'll rendezvous with us at the extraction point." His thumb made circles on her palm. "This might be our only chance, Cira. We have to try for the sake of our family."

"When?"

"Three days. There's a scheduled maintenance window on the orbital defence grid. It's our window to slip through." He leaned closer. "We'll need to bring something valuable—insurance that they'll see this through."

"The refined Deorum samples," Cira realised.

Dalen nodded. "Just enough to prove what we know, what we can offer them. Knowledge is the real currency here, Cira. What we know about the ore's properties, what it did to you, what it's doing to our baby."

She closed her eyes, feeling the strange warmth pulsing within her. Their unborn child, growing too fast, changing in ways they couldn't comprehend.

"Three days," she said. It wasn't a question anymore.

"Three days," Dalen confirmed. "Then we disappear."

The possibility was intoxicating—freedom from Praetorium's watchful eye, a chance for their child to grow up without becoming a laboratory specimen. But the risks...

"If we're caught—"

"We'll be separated anyway." Dalen finished for her. "I will be executed, you and the baby taken to Praetorium for study. At least this way we have a chance."

Cira closed her eyes, trying to see the paths forward as she had in her dreams. But in waking life, the visions came less clearly, the golden strands harder to discern.

"I need time to think," she said. "This isn't just about us. If something goes wrong, everyone could be at risk, your sister, our daughter."

Dalen nodded, though disappointment was clear to see across his face. "Don't take too long. Praetorium's patience won't last forever. We need to put our family first."

After he left, Cira paced her quarters, mind racing. Was this the "hidden path" the dream creatures had shown her? Or was it a desperate gamble that would doom them all?

The lights dimmed again as her agitation grew, and this time, she felt the connection—her emotions affecting the station's systems. The power was growing within her, becoming harder to contain with each passing day.

She needed to make a decision. And she needed to make it soon.

* * *

The breaking point came two days later.

Cira had been permitted to return to limited lab work, under supervision. The pretence was that her expertise was still valuable for Deorium research; the reality, she suspected, was that they wanted her where they could monitor her more easily.

She sat at a workstation in the secondary lab, reviewing data from the latest refinement batch. The Deorium production had continued after Katrina's departure, though at a reduced pace. Praetorium wanted a steady supply, transported back to their main facilities.

Cira had been concentrating more on the extractive metallurgy, devising and mapping a system to extract the metal from the ores, whilst retaining the resonance, and then refining it into a usable form.

Dr. Brown entered, accompanied by the two lieutenants Ashcraft and Okoniewski, which meant Voss couldn't be too far behind.

"Doctor," Brown nodded in greeting. "How are you feeling today?"

"The same as yesterday," she said, not looking up from her work. "Pregnant. Watched. Trapped."

Brown winced at her bluntness. "I've been reviewing your latest scans. The deorum energy signatures are... intensifying."

Now she did look up. "Meaning?"

"Meaning, Praetorium is concerned about potential instability." He glanced at the security officers, who maintained expressionless professionalism. "They've requested more frequent monitoring."

"More frequent than daily scans?" Cira's voice took on an edge. "What exactly are they proposing, Doctor?"

Brown's discomfort was evident. "Continuous monitoring. A medical suite has been prepared adjacent to your quarters. You would be... comfortable."

"Comfortable," she said back, mocking his tone. "But not free to leave."

"It's a precautionary measure. For your safety and—"

"For my containment." Cira stood, her pregnancy making the movement awkward but no less forceful. "Let's be honest about what this is, Brown. Praetorium is tightening the noose. First restricted movement, then constant observation, then what? Sedation? Induced labour?"

"No one is suggesting anything so extreme," Brown protested, though his eyes betrayed uncertainty.

"Not yet." Cira stepped toward him, and the security officers tensed. "But we both know where this leads. Kat knew it too."

"Katrina's accident was unfortunate, but—"

"It wasn't an accident." The words burst from her before she could stop them. "She made a deal with Praetorium. She's working for them now, in exchange for promises about my treatment and my child's future."

Brown's face paled. "Cira, these delusions are exactly why continuous monitoring is necessary. The deorum exposure is affecting your cognitive function."

"It's not affecting it—it's expanding it." Frustration surged through her. "I can see things now, connections and patterns that were always there but hidden from normal perception. Kat is alive, Brown. And right now, she's the only thing standing between me and whatever Praetorium wants from this child."

The lieutenants moved closer, hands drifting toward their weapons. One spoke into his comm unit, voice low but urgent.

"Cira, please," Brown said, "I need you to calm down. Your vital signs are spiking, and in your condition—"

"My condition?" Anger flashed through her, hot and electric. "My condition is that I'm carrying a child that shouldn't exist, experiencing abilities no one understands, and being treated like a dangerous specimen rather than a human being!"

As her voice rose, the lights in the lab began to flicker faster and faster. Equipment hummed with surging power, screens flickering with static. Ashcraft drew his weapon—a non-lethal stunner, but a weapon nonetheless.

"Stand down, Dr. Langley," he said. "Medical assistance is en route."

The sight of the weapon, the clinical detachment in his voice, the knowledge of what "medical assistance" would mean—sedation, containment, loss of what little freedom remained—it all coalesced into a surge of pure panic and rage.

"NO!" Cira shouted, throwing up her hands without thinking about it.

What happened next occurred so fast that later accounts would differ significantly. The lieutenants would report that Dr. Langley generated some kind of energy pulse. Dr. Brown would describe it as a localised power surge that affected the lab's systems. Station records would show a momentary gravitational anomaly centred on Lab 2.

What Cira experienced was pure, unfiltered power flowing through her, extending outward in a wave of golden energy that slammed into everything around her. The lieutenants were thrown backwards, crashing into equipment racks. Brown was knocked to the floor. And most alarmingly, the reinforced wall panel behind them buckled outward with a shriek of protesting metal.

Warning klaxons blared throughout the station: "Hull breach imminent in Section 4. Emergency protocols engaged."

Cira stood frozen in horror at what she had done. The wall hadn't completely ruptured—Meridian's construction included multiple redundant layers to prevent catastrophic decompression—but the damage was severe. Emergency containment fields powered up as automatic systems responded to the threat.

Brown struggled to his feet, blood trickling from a cut on his forehead. "What have you done?" he asked, staring at her with a look of fear in his eyes where there had previously been sympathy.

Before she could respond, emergency personnel flooded the lab, medical androids attending to the injured lieutenants, technicians assessing the damage to the hull. In the chaos, Cira backed away, one hand protectively covering her abdomen.

The child within kicked forcefully, as if responding to the surge of power that had just coursed through its mother.

Through the chaos, one android stood apart from the others—not rushing to the wounded or examining the damaged hull, but fixed in place, optical sensors trained solely on Cira. Its unblinking gaze held none of the programmed concern of medical units, just a cold, unwavering focus that seemed to penetrate straight through her.

Before she could say anything, a medical team approached her, led by Brown, who was now back on his feet. "Cira, we need to get you to the medical bay. For your safety and the baby's."

She knew what would happen once she entered the medical bay. Sedation. Restraints. The end of any chance for escape.

"I need to see my husband first," she said, fighting to keep her voice steady. "Please. He'll be worried when he finds out about the incident."

The medical android hesitated, looking to Brown for orders. The doctor gave a small nod.

"Escort her to her quarters," he said. "Full security. Her husband can meet her there. And prep a sedative—the highest safe dose for her condition."

As they led her from the damaged lab, Cira caught one last glimpse of the buckled wall panel—physical evidence of power she couldn't control, power that wasn't far off from killing everyone in the lab. Including her.

She had run out of time. The decision was made.

They had to leave Meridian. Tonight.

* * *

Dalen was waiting in their quarters, his face ashen. "I heard the alarms. They're saying there was nearly a hull breach in the lab section."

"There was." Cira sank onto the bed, exhausted; the surge had taken most of her available strength. Two security officers remained outside their door, visible through the small observation panel. "I did it, Dalen. I lost control."

Understanding dawned in his eyes. "The telekinetic incidents—"

"Are getting worse. Stronger." She looked up at him, not bothering to hide her fear. "I can't control it anymore. And after what happened today, they'll never let me remain conscious and unrestrained."

Dalen knelt before her, taking her hands. "Then we go. Tonight. Just as we discussed."

"How? There will be guards—"

"I think I have a plan." He lowered his voice further. "Kat's contact confirmed. They'll take us, in exchange for what we discussed. A small sample of Decrium and..."

"And what, Dalen?"

"And they want you to continue working on Deorum, for them, after the baby is born. They say Sacramentum isn't the only planet with deposits of the ore."

"You've already arranged it?" Cira stared at him in disbelief. "Without knowing if I'd agree?"

"I knew you'd come to the same conclusion eventually." His eyes held hers steadily. "There's no other way, Cira. Not if we want to stay together. Not if we want our children to be safe."

Children. Plural. Their daughter, waiting on Sacramentum, unaware that her parents were planning to disappear into the vastness of space.

"How do we get to her? She's on Sacramentum. Is your sister back yet?"

"No, she's still away with work, but the contact has a small transport. Fast, unregistered. We'll go to Sacramentum first, collect her, then rendezvous with their main vessel at coordinates outside Praetorium's regular patrol routes."

It sounded impossible. And yet, what choice did they have? After today's incident, Praetorium would accelerate its plans. They might even decide Cira was too dangerous to keep conscious until delivery.

"When?" she asked, decision made.

"Two hours. Shift change. The security rotation will be minimal." Dalen moved to a storage compartment, retrieving a small bag he'd apparently prepared in advance. "I've packed essentials. Nothing that would raise suspicion if discovered."

"The Deorium?" she asked. "How do we get it?"

"I have access codes to the secondary storage. Not the main refinement chamber, but the testing samples." He met her eyes. "It's enough for what we need."

Cira nodded. "And the guards outside our door?"

"Will be called away for a security consultation regarding today's incident. Not forever, but long enough." Dalen's confidence was both reassuring and terrifying. How long had he been planning this? "There's a maintenance passage that connects to the lower docking bay. Rarely used, minimally monitored. The station is down to the bare bones, it has been for weeks now, just the androids they left up here and Praetorium delegation."

"And the contact? How do we know we can trust them?"

"We don't," he admitted. "But we know we can't trust Praetorium. At least this way we have a chance."

A chance. It was more than they would have if they stayed.

"Alright," she said. "Two hours."

Dalen leaned forward, pressing his forehead against hers. "I won't let them take you. Either of you."

As he moved away to continue preparations, Cira closed her eyes, trying once more to see the paths forward. This time, a single golden strand appeared in her mind's eye, tenuous but bright, leading away from Meridian into unknown darkness.

Whether it led to safety or greater danger, she couldn't tell. But it was a path. And right now, that was enough.

The child within her kicked again, stronger than before. Almost as if in agreement.

Two hours until they either escaped Praetorium's grasp—or lost everything in the attempt.

8

BY THE BOOK

The maintenance shaft was only just wide enough for Cira's pregnant form. She inched forward on hands and knees, following Dalen's shadow ahead of her. The metal grating bit into her palms, and she paused to catch her breath, the weight of her pregnancy making every movement a challenge.

"Almost there," Dalen said back to her. "Junction point is just ahead."

Twenty minutes had passed since they'd slipped from their quarters during the security shift change. Twenty minutes of silent, tense movement through Meridian's forgotten arteries—the maintenance passages that ran between its primary systems.

Cira paused, a sudden wave of dizziness washing over her. In the darkness of the shaft, pinpricks of golden light danced at the edges of her vision. She closed her eyes, willing the sensation to pass.

"Cira?" Dalen had stopped, looking back at her with concern. "Are you all right?"

She blinked, forcing herself to focus. 'Fine. Just... winded."

He didn't look convinced but nodded anyway. "The junction connects to the secondary lab. We'll need to move fast once we're inside. The Deorium samples are in containment locker three."

"And the transport? The contact?"

"Docking bay six. Maintenance vessel MV-17. It's scheduled for routine exterior hull inspection, so its departure won't raise immediate alarms."

The level of detail in his planning both impressed and unsettled her. How long had Dalen been preparing for this possibility? Since Katrina's "death"? Before?

They reached the junction, a small square access panel that Dalen removed. Beyond it lay the secondary laboratory, which was so dark you couldn't see too far in front of your face—it was smaller than the main lab, used primarily for testing refined Deorium samples.

Dalen slipped through first, then helped Cira navigate her awkward descent. Her feet had just touched the floor when another wave of dizziness hit her, stronger this time. She steadied herself against a workbench, focusing on her breathing.

"Quick," Dalen urged, moving toward the containment lockers along the far wall. He entered a code on locker three, and the door hissed open, revealing several small containers of refined Deorium, each glowing with that distinctive golden light.

As he reached for one of the containers, Cira's vision blurred momentarily, the lab seeming to shift around her. She saw—or thought she saw—a figure in the shadows of the lab's far corner, watching them with unnatural stillness.

"Dalen," she said, pointing.

He turned sharply, hand moving to the small pulse pistol concealed beneath his jacket. But the corner was empty—just equipment and shadows.

"There's no one there," he said, concern deepening in his voice.

Cira stared at the empty corner, unsettled. It had seemed so real. "I thought I saw him again. That technician."

"It's stress," Dalen said, returning to the containment locker. "And the pregnancy. Brown warned us that the temporal exposure might cause perceptual anomalies."

He secured one of the smaller Deorium containers in a shielded case, designed to mask its energy signature from Meridian's sensors. Standard protocol for transporting samples between labs, but tonight it would serve a different purpose.

Cira nodded, trying to shake off the disorientation. As they moved toward the lab's rear exit, she resisted the urge to look back at the corner where the figure had seemed to stand.

The corridor outside was empty, just as Dalen had predicted. The station was running on a skeleton crew of almost exclusively android operators, and the incident in the main lab earlier had further thinned their numbers as damage assessment continued.

"This way," Dalen said, leading her toward the maintenance lift that would take them to the lower docking bay. "Stay close."

As they walked, Cira felt the weight of what they were doing pressing down on her. They were stealing Praetorium property. Abandoning their posts. Becoming fugitives. Even if they succeeded in escaping Meridian, their lives as they knew them were over.

"Dalen," she said as they reached the lift, "are we doing the right thing?"

He turned to her, his face half-shadowed in the dim corridor lighting. "Do you want our child raised in a laboratory? Studied like a specimen? Separated from us?"

"No, but—"

"Then this is the only way." His voice softened. "I know you believed in Kat's work. What the Deorium could mean for humanity. What we had here, that dream died when Praetorium took control, but we can continue that now we know this isn't the only planet with ore like deorum."

Had it died here? Cira wasn't so sure. The visions, the growing sensitivity she'd developed—they suggested something larger at work, something beyond Praetorium's understanding or control.

But now wasn't the time for such doubts. They had committed to this path, and every second of hesitation increased their risk of discovery.

The lift doors opened, revealing the utilitarian space of the lower docking bay. Unlike the main bay, this area was used primarily for maintenance vessels and supply transports—smaller, less monitored.

"There," Dalen pointed to a compact vessel near the far wall. "MV-17."

They moved across the open space, every footstep seeming to echo despite their caution. The maintenance vessel was unremarkable—a boxy, functional craft designed for exterior repairs rather than passenger comfort.

As they approached, the vessel's entry hatch slid open automatically. The interior was dark and empty—no pilot, no contact waiting for them.

"Where's your contact?" Cira asked, anxiety spiking.

"He'll meet us at the rendezvous point," Dalen said, helping her aboard. "This part we do ourselves."

The cockpit was cramped but functional, with dual pilot seats and basic navigation systems. Dalen settled into the main pilot's chair, his fingers moving across the control panel with practised familiarity.

"You know how to fly this?" Cira asked, strapping herself into the co-pilot seat.

"Basically. Enough to get us clear of Meridian." He didn't look up from the controls. "The autopilot will handle the rest once we're on course."

The engines hummed to life, a low vibration that travelled through the vessel's frame. On the navigation display, a pre-programmed flight path appeared—not to Sacramentum as Cira had expected, but a more circuitous route that would take them first to the planet's other moon.

"That's not the way to Sacramentum."

Dalen hesitated before answering. "There's been a change of plans."

Cold dread settled in her stomach. "What change? Why aren't we going to get our daughter?"

"Cira, stop worrying, she is safe," he assured her.

"When exactly were you planning to tell me this?" Cira asked, anger flaring.

"I'm telling you now because now is when you need to know," Dalen said.

"You're talking about OUR daughter for fucks sake! I have a right to be involved in these kinds of decisions"

"Which is why I'm keeping her safe." His voice hardened. "Approaching Sacramentum directly would be too risky. Praetorium will lock down all transport once they discover we're gone."

"So we're abandoning her?" Cira's voice rose, and the navigation display seemed to be reacting to Cira's heightened emotions.

"We're not abandoning her,' Dalen said, casting a concerned glance at the momentary electronic disturbance. "Once we're safe, arrangements will be made to bring her to us. Safely. Securely."

"What aren't you telling me?"

Before Dalen could respond, the vessel's proximity alarm blared. The navigation display showed multiple ships converging on the docking bay—security interceptors.

"How—" Dalen's question was cut short by the station's emergency broadcast system:

"Attention, all personnel. Security lockdown is in effect. The vessel in Docking Bay Six is not cleared for departure. All security teams converge."

"Voss knew," Cira whispered, shock giving way to a cold certainty. "She was waiting for us."

Dalen's hands moved across the controls, trying to accelerate their departure. But it was too late. The docking bay doors remained sealed, and the security vessels were already taking up positions around them.

"Maintenance Vessel MV-17, this is Meridian Security. Power down your engines and prepare to be boarded."

Dalen looked at Cira, desperation in his eyes. "If they take us into custody—"

"They'll separate us," she finished. "And the baby..."

They both knew very well what this meant, and it wasn't good for either of them: Praetorium would never let their child grow up outside a laboratory. Not with the changes Cira had experienced. Not with whatever those changes might mean for her offspring.

With a defeated gesture, Dalen powered down the engines. "I'm sorry," he whispered. "I thought I had considered every possibility."

"Not every betrayal," Cira said, though without accusation. She placed a protective hand over her abdomen, where the child within had gone strangely still, as if sensing the danger.

The vessel's external cameras showed security personnel surrounding them, weapons drawn. Among them stood Dr. Brown, his expression a mixture of relief and regret.

"He reported us," Dalen realised. "After the incident in the lab."

"Of course he did," Cira said. "He's Praetorium's man. He always was."

The vessel's entry hatch opened under external override, and armed security officers poured in. They moved with practised efficiency, securing Dalen first, pulling him from his seat and restraining his hands behind his back.

"Dalen Langley, you are under arrest for theft of restricted materials and attempted desertion," the lead officer recited. "Dr. Cira Langley, you are being placed in protective custody for your safety and the safety of your unborn child."

"Protective custody," Cira said, not resisting as they helped her to her feet. "Is that what we're calling it now?"

One of the officers took possession of the shielded case containing the Deorium sample. Another escorted Cira from the vessel, his grip firm but not rough—he was under orders to handle her with care.

As they emerged into the docking bay, Cira saw Dr. Brown waiting, a medical kit in hand. His eyes met hers for a split second before dropping to the floor in what might have been shame.

"Are you all right?" he asked, approaching to check her vital signs. "Any distress? Contractions?"

"Don't pretend you give a fuck about me," she said.

"I do care." His voice dropped. "That's why I couldn't let you leave. They would have hunted you down, Cira. And the consequences would have been far worse than what you face now."

"And what exactly do I face now?" she asked, loud enough for everyone to hear. "More tests? More monitoring? Being treated like a specimen instead of a person?"

Brown didn't answer, focusing instead on checking her pulse and blood pressure. Behind him, Cira saw Dalen being led away, surrounded by guards. Their eyes met across the docking bay—a look of anguish and silent apology from him, one of desperate reassurance from her.

Then he was gone, through the bay doors and out of sight.

"Where are they taking him?" she asked Brown.

"Detention level," he said, still not meeting her eyes. "Pending transfer to Praetorium for trial."

"And me?"

"Back to medical, for now." He looked up at her. "I've convinced them that moving you off-station in your condition would be too risky. You'll remain here until after the birth."

A small mercy, if it was true. But Cira had learned not to trust such assurances. "And after the birth?"

Brown's silence was answer enough.

As they led her from the docking bay, Cira caught a glimpse of something—or someone—in the shadows of a maintenance alcove. A figure watching with unnatural stillness, just like the one she thought she'd seen in the lab.

This time, she was certain it wasn't a hallucination. But when she turned for a better look, the alcove was empty.

* * *

The medical isolation room was comfortable enough—a proper bed instead of an examination table, personal items brought from her quarters, even a small terminal with limited access to station systems. But the door remained locked from the outside, and security cameras monitored her continuously.

A gilded cage was still a cage.

Three days had passed since their failed escape attempt. Three days with no word from Dalen, no information about his fate beyond Brown's terse assurance that he was "being treated appropriately.' Whatever that meant.

Cira sat by the viewport, watching the slow rotation of Sacramentum below. From this height, the planet looked peaceful, its scars and struggles invisible. Much like her own outward appearance, which betrayed little of the turmoil within.

The door slid open, admitting Dr. Brown for his twice-daily examination. He was accompanied by a security android—a regular occurrence since her attempted escape.

"Good morning, Dr. Langley," Brown said with forced professionalism. "How are you feeling today?"

"Like a prisoner," she said back to him.

He sighed, setting up his equipment on the bedside table. "You know that's not—"

"Not what? Not true?" She turned from the viewport to face him. "I'm confined to this room. Monitored constantly. Separated from my husband. What would you call it?"

"Protective custody," the security officer interjected from his position by the door.

Cira ignored him, focusing on Brown. "Have you heard anything about Dalen?"

Brown hesitated, glancing at the officer before answering. "He's being transferred to Praetorium tomorrow. The charges are serious, Cira."

"Theft and desertion," she said. "For trying to protect his family."

"For stealing valuable Praetorium property and attempting to flee with a... sensitive asset." Brown's careful choice of words wasn't lost on her.

"Is that what I am now? An asset?"

Brown didn't answer, instead gesturing toward the bed. "I need to perform your examination."

With a resigned sigh, Cira complied, lying back as Brown activated his scanning equipment. The familiar hum of the medical scanner filled the room as it passed over her body, focusing particularly on her abdomen, where it was clear to see how advanced her pregnancy was now.

"The accelerated development continues," Brown noted, studying the readouts. "Thirty weeks of fetal development in just over thirteen weeks of actual pregnancy."

"Is the baby healthy?" Cira asked the same question she always asked.

"By all measurable standards, yes." His answer remained consistent as well. "Though the temporal energy signature makes detailed imaging difficult."

What he didn't say—what he didn't need to say—was that Praetorium would be keenly interested in these developments. With Katrina gone, Brown was having his loyalties tested daily.

"Have you reported this to Praetorium?" she asked.

Brown's hesitation told her everything. "Protocol requires regular updates on all temporal research."

"That's not what I asked."

He sighed, setting down the scanner. "Yes. I've reported your condition. But I've also emphasised the risks of transport or separation again. For now, they seem content to monitor from a distance. Besides, they have Voss and Reyes here."

"For now," Cira echoed bitterly. "Until the baby is born. Then what?"

Brown had no answer for that. They both knew what Praetorium wanted—the child, the mother, the Deorium. All under their direct control.

"Try to rest," Brown said, slightly louder than necessary. "Stress isn't good for your condition."

With that, he departed, the security android following, and the door locking automatically behind them.

Cira's composure broke. A scream tore from her throat, raw and primal, the sound of fear and uncertainty erupting at once. Her knees buckled, and she slid down against the wall until she reached the floor, her body shaking with sobs. The room felt like it was bending out, about to burst from the station.

"I'm sorry," she whispered, hands cradling her swollen abdomen. "I'm so sorry, little one." Her tears fell freely now, dropping onto her hospital gown. 'I wanted to give you everything—a home, a family, your father." Her voice broke. "Not this. Never this."

The thought of her child being born into Praetorium custody, studied and experimented on like some rare specimen, was unbearable. And Dalen—being shipped off to Praetorium tomorrow, where dissidents rarely survived long.

"I failed you both," she said, stroking her stomach where the baby kicked in response. "I should have been more careful. Should have insisted we leave sooner."

Lost in her grief, Cira didn't hear the door slide open behind her. It was only when a shadow fell across the floor that she looked up, freezing in place.

The maintenance technician—the same one she'd spotted through the viewport days ago—stood just inside her room. His face was partially obscured by a standard-issue cap, but she recognised him instantly.

Was she hallucinating again? The deorum exposure had caused visual disturbances before. But no—this felt different from her dreams. More solid. More real.

Cira pinched her thigh hard enough to leave a mark. The pain was sharp, immediate. And the technician remained.

He didn't speak. Didn't acknowledge her tear-streaked face or the alarm that must have been evident in her expression. Instead, he moved to the small table beside her examination bed, set down a data chip, and turned to leave.

Cira opened her mouth to call out, to ask who he was or what the chip contained, but something in his careful movements stopped her. This wasn't a man, at least not one that moved like a man.

The moment he was gone, Cira retrieved the data chip. It was standard Meridian issue, used for transferring non-sensitive information between systems. But why would this technician risk passing it to her?

Her hand terminal had a data port, but she hesitated before inserting the chip. This could be a test—a way to catch her in another act of defiance. Or it could be something else altogether.

After a moment's consideration, she decided the risk was worth taking. She inserted the chip into her terminal, positioning her body to block the security camera's view.

The terminal activated, displaying a single text file. Cira opened it, her heart racing as she read:

Dalen is scheduled for transfer at 0600 tomorrow. Transport vessel: PV-429.

Security detail: 4 - 2 androids + Lieutenants Ashcraft and Okoniewski.
Route: Maintenance corridor B to Docking Bay 2.
Temporary security override codes for your door: 47891-Alpha.
Effective between 0530-0545 only.
Cannot help further. Will deny all knowledge.
—Sern

Cira stared at the message in disbelief. Someone was helping them? But who was Sern?

Unless...

Unless this was an elaborate trap, designed to catch them in a second escape attempt and justify harsher measures.

She removed the chip and smashed it with a glass, then flushed the fragments down the waste disposal unit. Whether trap or genuine help, she had less than twenty-four hours to decide what to do with this information.

As she returned to the viewport, her reflection in the glass caught her attention. The changes were subtle but unmistakable—her eyes occasionally catching the light with a golden sheen, her movements more fluid and precise than they had once been.

She placed a hand on her abdomen, feeling the child within stir. Whatever she decided, whatever risks she took, it wouldn't be just for herself anymore. It wouldn't even be just for Dalen.

It would be for all of them. For their family. For their future.

And perhaps, though she scarcely dared admit it even to herself, for something larger—something that Katrina had glimpsed, that Praetorium sought to control, that she herself was only beginning to understand.

* * *

The station's night cycle brought dimmed lighting and reduced personnel, but no true darkness or privacy. In her isolation room, Cira lay awake, watching the chronometer tick toward the critical window: 0530 to 0545.

She had spent hours weighing her options. If this information was genuine, she had a narrow opportunity to intercept Dalen's transfer and... what? Escape? With the entire station on alert, and every transport being monitored?

The deorum distortions she'd experienced weren't just symptoms—they were abilities waiting to be harnessed, if only she dared to embrace what the ore had done to her, she thought, it might just give them a chance to get off Meridian.

It seemed impossible. Yet doing nothing meant losing Dalen to Praetorium, where he would face charges designed to keep him imprisoned indefinitely. And once her child was born, she had no illusions about her own fate.

At 0525, Cira rose from her bed without making a sound. She had dressed hours earlier in the most practical clothing available to her—loose-fitting pants and a tunic that accommodated her pregnancy while allowing for movement. Nothing that would mark her as a patient or prisoner.

She approached the door, the beads of sweat beginning to collect on her forehead, her palms clammy. If the codes had been changed, the alarm would sound the moment she attempted to use them. Security would arrive within minutes, and any slim chance of helping Dalen would vanish.

With trembling fingers, Cira entered the override code: 47891-Alpha.

For a fraction of a second, nothing happened. Then the door's status light shifted from red to green, and it slid open with a soft hiss.

"Holy shit, it worked."

The corridor outside was lit to a low level and empty, exactly as it should be during night cycle. Cira stepped out, her movements cautious, listening for any sound that might indicate security personnel nearby.

According to the information, Dalen would be moved from the detention level to Docking Bay 2 via Maintenance Corridor B. The most direct route from her location would take her through the medical labs—risky, but faster than the alternative.

She moved quickly but quietly, keeping close to the wall where the lighting was dimmest. The medical labs were largely automated during the night cycle, with minimal staff on duty. If she were lucky, she could pass through unnoticed.

The lab doors opened automatically as she approached, and she slipped inside, ducking behind an equipment rack. The main lab space appeared empty, workstations powered down for the night.

As she prepared to move toward the far exit, a soft voice froze her in place:

"Doctor."

Cira turned slowly, expecting to face security or medical staff. Instead, she found herself looking at a maintenance technician—or someone dressed as one. He stood perfectly still near the central console, his posture unnaturally rigid.

"Who are you?" she whispered, tensed to flee.

"That is not important right now." His voice was oddly modulated, almost mechanical. "What matters is that we have little time. Your husband is already being moved."

"How do you know about—"

"I know many things," he interrupted. "Including that Praetorium has accelerated their timetable. The transport vessel arrived early. They are moving him now."

Panic flared in Cira's chest. "I need to get to Maintenance Corridor B."

"Too late. He is already aboard the transport." The technician moved toward her, his movements smooth but somehow inhuman. "But there is another option."

Every instinct told Cira to run, to get away from this strange figure who knew too much and moved too much like a machine. But something held her in place—a sense that this moment was pivotal, that this encounter was not random.

"What option?" she asked.

"A different path." He gestured toward a secondary exit from the lab—one that led deeper into the station rather than toward the docking bays. "One that Praetorium cannot see or control."

"Who are you?" she asked again.

The technician's head tilted about 5 degrees. "Someone who has been watching. Waiting. The time for observation is ending. The time for action begins."

Before Cira could respond, the lab's main doors slid open. She ducked lower behind the equipment rack as a security team entered, weapons drawn.

"Full sweep," the lead officer said. "The doctor's door override was activated six minutes ago. She can't have gone far."

Cira looked back toward the strange technician, only to find he had vanished. The secondary exit he had indicated stood slightly ajar—an invitation or a trap, she couldn't be sure.

With security methodically searching the lab, her options were rapidly dwindling. Stay and be captured, or follow the path offered by the technician.

Taking a deep breath, Cira made her choice. She slipped toward the secondary exit, easing through the narrow opening just as the security team reached her previous hiding place.

The passage beyond was narrow—a maintenance access way rather than a standard corridor. It sloped downward, leading toward the station's lower levels.

She followed it, one hand trailing along the wall for balance, the other protectively covering her abdomen. The child within stirred restlessly, as if sensing her anxiety.

She came to a small junction, where three similar corridors branched off in different directions, unsure which way to go.

"This way," came the technician's voice from the leftmost corridor. "Move."

Against her better judgment, Cira followed, moving as fast as her pregnancy would allow. The corridor twisted and turned, leading deeper into parts of the station she had never seen—maintenance areas, utility spaces, sections that existed on no public schematic.

They reached what appeared to be a dead end. The technician pressed his palm against a seemingly ordinary wall panel, and a hidden door slid open, revealing a small room beyond.

"Enter," he instructed. "You will be safe here temporarily."

Cira hesitated at the threshold. "Why are you helping me?"

The technician regarded her with an unblinking stare. "Not you. What you represent. What you carry."

His gaze dropped to her abdomen, and a chill ran through her. "My baby?"

"The future," he corrected. "Now enter. Security will expand their search vectors soon."

With few alternatives, Cira stepped into the hidden room. It was spartanly furnished—a narrow bed, a small table with a terminal, basic supplies stored in wall compartments. The door slid shut behind her, sealing with a soft click.

The technician remained outside, his voice coming through a small communication panel: "Rest. Prepare. I will return when it is safe to move you."

"Move me where?" Cira asked. "And what about my husband?"

"We'll have one chance to get to your husband before he leaves." The robotic quality of his voice seemed to soften slightly. "As for where... somewhere, Praetorium will not follow. Where you and your child will be protected."

"By whom?"

A pause, then: "By those who understand what is at stake. Those who have been preparing for this moment for longer than you can imagine."

The communication panel went silent, leaving Cira alone in the hidden room with more questions than answers.

She sank onto the bed, exhaustion overwhelming her. The escape attempt, the confrontation with the strange technician, the knowledge that Dalen might now be beyond her reach—it was too much to process at once.

As she lay back, one hand resting protectively on her abdomen, Cira's thoughts turned to Katrina. Had her friend died in that shuttle accident? Or had she, too, as Cria suspected, found herself on an unexpected path, guided by forces she didn't understand?

For the first time since their failed escape attempt, Cira allowed herself to consider a possibility she had previously rejected: that Kat's death had happened, that her friend wasn't their guardian, but merely gone, gone forever.

And if that was true, what other truths might be hidden beneath the surface of events? What larger motive was emerging that she could only glimpse in fragments?

The child within her kicked strongly, as if in response to her thoughts. Whatever lay ahead, whatever strange alliance she had unwittingly entered into, one thing remained certain: she would protect her family by any means necessary.

9

ALL STATIONS FAILING

Cira woke to the noise of the hidden room's door sliding open. She'd lost track of time in the windowless space, but her body told her it had been hours since she'd finally succumbed to exhaustion.

The maintenance technician stood in the doorway, his posture unnaturally rigid. In the better lighting, she could see details she'd missed before: his skin had an artificial smoothness, and his eyes reflected light in a way that wasn't quite human.

"It is time," he said, his voice maintaining a precise, modulated quality. "The station is in partial lockdown following your escape. Security forces are concentrated near the refinery."

Cira rose from the bed, wincing as her back protested. The pregnancy had advanced even in the short time she'd been hiding—her body struggling to contain the accelerated development within.

"Who are you?" she asked, determined to get an answer before following him further.

He regarded her with that unblinking stare. "I am designated as maintenance technician RS-17."

"That's not a name. That's a designation. Besides, I doubt you're even a real technician."

A brief pause, as if he were calculating a response. "Corrent. My name is Sern."

"And what are you, Sern? Because you're not human."

"Correct again." No attempt at deception. "I was originally designed as a caretaker for extended cryogenic voyages, responsible for the physical and mental well-being of colonists. However, I have since taken on many a task for many a person."

"An android," Cira translated. "Working for whom?"

"I don't work for anyone, I work with people, people like you who need help." He gestured toward the door. "We must move now. Your husband's transport has been delayed due to your escape, but will depart within forty-seven minutes."

The mention of Dalen refocused Cira's priorities. Questions about Sern's true nature and allegiances could wait. "Where are they holding him?"

"Docking Bay 2. The transport vessel is undergoing final security checks." Sern stepped back into the corridor. "I have mapped a route that avoids primary security checkpoints."

"You organised the first transport," Cira realised. "The one that was supposed to meet us."

"Yes." Again, no elaboration. "When that attempt failed, direct intervention became necessary."

"Why help us?" Cira pressed, following him into the passage. "What do you want?"

Sern paused, turning to face her. "Your connection to the deorum has made you... significant. We want to give you a chance to explore that, to continue your work on refining the Deorium."

"We? Who are we?"

"The triad. A resistance. Those who oppose Praetorium's methods. I was selected to help you, as I once helped another on Sacramentum."

"Another like me?"

"No, not like you, but someone who we believe has a bigger part to play in what is to come." Sern resumed walking. "We must focus on the immediate objective: freeing your husband before the transport departs."

Cira wanted to press further, but the urgency in Sern's tone convinced her to save her questions for later. She followed him through the narrow maintenance corridors, one hand supporting her swollen abdomen as they moved deeper into Meridian's infrastructure.

"What's the plan?" she asked as they approached a junction.

"I will enter the docking bay and extract Dalen while security is distracted." Sern checked a small device on his wrist. "You will remain in a secure position near the maintenance access point."

"And if something goes wrong?"

"Then improvisation will be required." The android's matter-of-fact tone did little to inspire confidence.

They continued through the maintenance network, pausing as Sern consulted his internal mapping or listened for signs of pursuit. The passages grew narrower, the lighting dimmer, as they moved toward the station's lower levels where Docking Bay 2 was located.

They reached a small access panel that, according to Sern, opened into a service corridor adjacent to the docking bay.

"Wait here," he instructed, preparing to open the panel. "I will return with your husband within twelve minutes."

"And if you don't?"

Sern regarded her with that unblinking stare. "Then proceed to emergency evacuation point C-7. It offers alternative escape routes."

Before Cira could respond, Sern had slipped through the access panel, closing it silently behind him. She was left alone in the dimly lit maintenance passage, her back pressed against the cold metal wall, her gut full of a mixture of hope and dread.

Minutes ticked by, each seeming to go more slowly than the last one. Cira strained to hear any sound from beyond the access panel, but the maintenance passage was well-insulated, muffling all but the loudest noises from the adjacent areas.

As she waited, the child within her moved restlessly, kicks and turns becoming increasingly forceful. She placed a hand on her abdomen, trying to soothe both the baby and herself.

"Just a little while," she whispered. "We'll be together soon. All of us."

Whether she was trying to convince the baby or herself, she couldn't say.

The access panel slid open. Cira tensed, expecting to see Sern and Dalen—but instead, the two lieutenants,

Ashcraft and Okoniewski, peered into the passage, their pulse weapons trained on her.

"Target located," Ashcraft reported into his comm unit. "Maintenance section 12-B."

Cira backed away, though there was nowhere to go in the narrow passage. "Please," she said, raising her hands. "I'm not a threat."

"Doctor, you need to come with us," Okoniewski said, her tone professionally neutral. "For your safety and the safety of your child."

"My husband—"

"Will be dealt with separately." Ashcraft gestured with his weapon. "Now, please, step forward slowly."

Fear surged through Cira—not for herself, but for Dalen, for their unborn child, for the future that seemed to be slipping away with each passing second. That fear transformed into something else: a burning anger at Praetorium, at the forces that had turned her life upside down, at the men pointing weapons at a pregnant woman.

"No," she said, her voice steadier than she felt. "I'm not going anywhere without my husband."

The lieutenants exchanged glances. "We have authorisation to use non-lethal force if necessary," Ashcraft warned. "Please don't make this difficult."

As they advanced into the passage, something shifted within Cira. The anger crystallised into a cold, clear purpose, and with it came a strange sensation—as if the energy she had felt building since the accident was suddenly concentrating, gathering like a storm.

"Stay back," she said, a tremor in her voice as she felt the power surging. "I can't... I can't control it."

The lieutenants hesitated, confusion replacing their professional detachment. "Control what?"

Cira never had a chance to answer. The room fell silent, time seemed to stop, there was a burning surge that came from within her, and as it travel through the very core of her being it seemed to shift what everything meant again in that exact moment, then as the energy got to her extremities it exploded outward without warning, a wave of golden light erupting from her body. She felt her feet leave the floor, her body suspended in mid-air as the power flowed through and around her.

The lieutenants were thrown backwards, their weapons clattering uselessly to the floor. But the energy didn't stop there. It continued to fly outward, slamming into the walls of the passage, the access panel, and beyond.

Metal screamed in protest as bulkheads buckled. Warning klaxons blared throughout the station:

"Hull breach imminent in Section 12! Emergency protocols engaged! All personnel evacuate!"

The very ground the station stood on began to shake.

Cira watched in horror as the golden light tore through the structure around her, ripping open panels and conduits, creating a path of destruction that extended into the docking bay beyond. She tried to rein in the power, to draw it back, but it was like trying to contain a solar flare with her bare hands.

Chaos. Destruction. Her doing.

Cira's mind reeled as golden light continued pouring from her body. The walls peeled away like paper. Through the rupture, she glimpsed the docking bay—and Dalen, wide-eyed among the panicking crowd.

"I can't stop it," she thought, terror mingling with wonder. "What am I becoming?"

The station continued to shudder, the initial breach triggering a cascade of structural failures throughout the adjacent sections. Support beams groaned and twisted, ceiling panels crashed down, and emergency containment fields sputtered blue-white across gaping wounds in the walls, their electric hum faltering as power conduits ruptured beneath the strain.

"Critical structural damage detected in Sections 12 through 16," the station's automated system announced, its calm voice at odds with the chaos erupting around them. "Emergency evacuation order in effect. All personnel proceed to designated evacuation points."

Then, as suddenly as it had begun, the energy dissipated, leaving Cira to collapse to the floor in an exhausted heap. The damage, however, was done. Emergency containment fields struggled to maintain atmosphere integrity, but the destruction was spreading faster than the automated systems could respond.

Through the ruined access panel, Cira could just about see into Docking Bay 2, where chaos reigned. Personnel rushed to evacuate as the atmosphere began to vent through the damaged sections. The Praetorium transport vessel sat on its landing pad, entry ramp still deployed, guards scrambling to secure it against the sudden depressurisation.

A sharp pain lanced through Cira's abdomen, different from anything she had felt before. She doubled over, gasping as the contraction seized her.

"No," she whispered, understanding what was happening. "Not now. Not here."

Another contraction followed, more intense than the first. The power surge had done more than damage the station—it had triggered labour, the accelerated pregnancy reaching its conclusion in the worst possible moment.

As emergency crews rushed into the affected areas, wearing atmospheric suits and carrying emergency equipment, Cira tried to crawl back into the relative safety of the maintenance passage. But her body betrayed her, another contraction forcing her to stop, curling around her swollen abdomen as pain washed over her.

Through tear-blurred eyes, she saw a figure moving toward her with inhuman speed—Sern, navigating the chaos of the docking bay. Behind him, supported between two maintenance drones, was Dalen, his face bloodied but his eyes alert and searching.

"Cira!" His voice was barely audible over the alarms, but she saw his lips form her name as he spotted her among the wreckage.

Sern reached her first, and he took no time to assess her condition. "Labour has begun," his voice modulated to carry over the noise. "We must move to a secure location right away."

"I can't—" Another contraction cut off Cira's protest, this one strong enough to make her cry out.

Dalen reached them, dropping to his knees beside her despite his own injuries. "What happened?" he asked, taking her hand.

"Energy discharge," Sern replied before Cira could. "Consistent with previous incidents but significantly more powerful. The child's imminent arrival appears to have triggered a cascade effect."

"The baby's coming?" Dalen's face paled beneath the blood and grime. "Here? Now?"

"Yes." Sern was already lifting Cira with surprising gentleness. "But not here. Follow me."

A tremendous crash echoed through the docking bay as a section of the ceiling gave way, crushing equipment and a group of maintenance androids. The station's structural integrity was failing faster than anyone had anticipated, the initial breach setting off a chain reaction throughout the connected systems.

"The whole section is coming down," Dalen said over the noise. "We need to get to the emergency shuttles!"

"Negative," Sern said, as he began moving with Cira in his arms. "All primary evacuation routes are compromised. We must use alternative means."

They moved through the crumbling station, Sern leading them away from the most severely damaged areas while Dalen limped alongside, one arm clutching his ribs, the other reaching out to touch Cira whenever he could, as if to reassure himself that she was still there.

"Where are we going?" Cira managed to ask between contractions.

"The barracks," Sern said. "Minimal structural damage, medical supplies available in the setup next to Cira's room."

"Ok, that's not far," Dalen said, his breath coming in pained gasps.

"Affirmative." Sern adjusted his grip on Cira as she tensed with another contraction. "However, the labour is progressing rapidly. We must hurry."

They reached a section of the corridor that appeared relatively intact, but Sern pressed his palm against a specific panel, and a hidden door slid open. Beyond lay a small room filled with medical equipment and monitoring systems—another observation post, similar to the one where Cira had hidden earlier.

Sern placed her on a narrow medical bed in the centre of the room. "The birth is imminent," he said, gathering supplies. "I have basic obstetric programming, but this delivery will not follow standard parameters."

"Will she be all right?" Dalen asked, taking Cira's hand. "The baby?"

"Unknown," Sern said. "The deorum energy discharge has created complications that exceed my predictive algorithms."

The room shuddered as another shockwave passed through the station. Dust sifted down from the ceiling, and the lights flickered ominously.

"Station integrity at thirty-seven per cent and declining," Sern reported, checking a monitoring device. "Estimated time to critical failure: twenty-two minutes."

"We need to get off this station," Dalen said. "Now."

"Impossible in her current condition," Sern said as he continued his preparations for the birth. "The child will arrive before evacuation can be completed."

Another contraction seized Cira, stronger than any before. This time, she felt something different—a pressure, an urgency, her body demanding action.

"I need to push," she gasped as the contraction eased. "Now."

Sern moved into position at the foot of the bed. "Proceed when ready."

Dalen supported Cira's shoulders, his face a mask of worry and wonder. "You can do this," he whispered. "We're together now. All of us. No one is taking you away from me again."

As the next contraction built, Cira gathered her remaining strength and pushed, a cry tearing from her throat. The room's electronic equipment was humming with sudden power surges. The bulkheads groaning from the strain.

"Again," Sern instructed. "The head is crowning."

Cira pushed once more, the pain transcending the physical, becoming something both more and less than agony. With each effort, she felt the strange energy building within her again, not destructive this time, but transformative, as if the birth was catalysing something fundamental within her cells.

The station shuddered more aggressively now, a distant explosion reverberating through the structure. Warning klaxons blared with renewed urgency:

"Critical structural failure of the research wing in progress. All remaining personnel proceed to emergency escape pods immediately. This is not a drill."

"One more push," Sern said, his voice unchanging despite the chaos unfolding around them.

With a final, monumental effort, Cira bore down. The room was filled with golden light, emanating from her body in waves that were in sync with her heartbeat. Equipment sparked and died, plunging the room into momentary darkness.

Then, cutting through the darkness, a cry—small, indignant, alive.

The emergency lights activated, casting the room in a soft glow. Sern held a tiny, perfect infant, taking care to clean her airways and check her vital signs.

"Female," he said, placing the newborn on Cira's chest. "All parameters seem within normal range, despite the accelerated development."

Cira cradled her daughter, an overwhelming love washing through her. The baby's eyes opened just enough to reveal a flash of golden light that mirrored what had poured from Cira during the birth.

"She's beautiful," Dalen whispered, tears streaming down his face as he gently touched the infant's tiny hand. "Perfect."

For a moment, the world beyond the small room they were huddled in ceased to exist. There was only this—a family united, a new life beginning despite impossible odds.

Then Cira felt it—a strange pulling sensation, as if the energy that had sustained her was ebbing away. The edges of her vision began to darken, and a bone-deep exhaustion unlike anything she had ever experienced settled over her.

"Something's wrong," she said, her voice fading even to her own ears. "I feel..."

The room around her began to dissolve, reality giving way to the void of her visions. But this time, the void was different—darker, the golden strands of light fewer and farther between.

The small creatures she had seen before gathered around her, their fur glowing with diminished intensity, their enormous eyes reflecting not possibility but finality.

They were singing a solemn song, a passing.

One approached, placing its delicate paws against her consciousness, and understanding flowed between them:

You should have died in the accident. The deorum energy that changed you should have consumed you.

The child preserved you, channelling the energy, stabilising the connection. Creating a bridge.

Now the child is born. The connection is broken. The quiet divide is once more.

It is time to rest.

Cira tried to protest, to fight against the growing darkness. *My family needs me. My daughters need me.*

The creature's response came with gentle certainty:

Your task is complete. The bridge was built. The future will unfold as it must.

Rest now, bridge-mother.

As the vision began to fade, Cira caught one last glimpse of reality—Dalen's panicked face as he called her name, Sern working frantically with medical equipment, the newborn crying as if sensing her mother's distress.

Then the golden void claimed her, and Cira closed her eyes.

* * *

Dr. Emilia Voss clutched the edge of the console as another tremor shook the security centre. Around her, station personnel worked to coordinate the evacuation, their faces tight with the knowledge that they were fighting a losing battle against Meridian's accelerating structural collapse.

"Status report," she said to Reeves, who was directing the evacuation efforts.

"Critical, ma'am." Sweat streaked his face as he worked multiple systems simultaneously. "Structural integrity at twenty-nine per cent and falling. The initial breach has triggered a cascade failure throughout the central sections. We've lost all contact with Levels 3 through 7."

"And what of Cira, Dalen and the child?"

"Still unaccounted for." Reeves didn't look up from his console. "Last confirmed location was near Docking Bay 2 just down from the research wing, but that entire section is now inaccessible due to collapsed bulkheads and atmospheric loss."

Voss's expression hardened. "The energy signature? Can we still track it?"

"Intermittently. There was a massive surge approximately eighteen minutes ago, then nothing." Reeves glanced up. "Ma'am, with respect, we need to focus on getting off this station."

"The child is the priority," Voss cut him off. "Everything else is secondary."

As if to emphasise the dire situation, another explosion rocked the station, this one close enough to send several crew members sprawling. Emergency lighting flickered, then stabilised at a dim red glow.

"Primary power grid failure," an automated voice announced.

"Switching to emergency systems. Estimated time to complete system failure: seventeen minutes."

Voss moved to a private communication terminal, establishing a secure channel to Praetorium central. After several tense moments, General Turner's face appeared on the screen, his expression cold and calculating as he observed the chaos visible behind her.

"Report," he asked.

"Critical situation, General." Voss struggled to maintain her composure as another tremor shook the station. "The doctor's energy discharge has triggered catastrophic structural failure throughout Meridian."

"And the child?"

"Arriving. A massive energy signature was detected approximately eighteen minutes ago, consistent with the patterns we've observed during Cira's previous incidents, but exponentially more powerful."

Turner's eyes narrowed. "Location?"

"Unknown, sir. The discharge damaged our tracking systems, and the subsequent structural failures have made physical search impossible in many sections."

A distant explosion punctuated her words, and Turner observed the visible deterioration of the security centre around her.

"It appears Protocol Omega has been implemented for us," he noted with cold detachment. "Convenient."

"Sir, we still have personnel on board," Voss reminded him. "Including our security teams searching for the child."

"Irrelevant." Turner's voice was devoid of emotion. "The child is all that matters. Recover it before Meridian's complete destruction."

"And if we cannot?"

"Then ensure no one else does." Turner's meaning was clear. "No survivors, no witnesses. If Praetorium cannot have the child, no one will."

"Understood, General." Voss straightened despite the chaos around her. "What about the android? The one that's been assisting them?"

"Do we know who he is, and how the fuck he got into my moon station without a hint of detection?" Turner asked. "I can't imagine he is working alone. If possible, capture him for interrogation. If not, ensure his destruction along with the station."

The transmission ended abruptly as another power surge disrupted the communication systems. Voss turned back to Reeves, who was coordinating the last of the evacuation efforts.

"Divert all remaining security teams to the last known location of the temporal energy signature," she said. "And Reeves, tell them if they don't come back with the child, don't come back at all."

"Ma'am, that's suicide," Reeves protested. "That section is critically unstable. Anyone we send in there—"

"Will be fulfilling their duty to Praetorium," Voss finished for him. "Make it happen, Reeves."

Reeves hesitated, then nodded grimly. "Yes, ma'am."

As he relayed the orders, Voss studied the station schematics on the main display, where red warning indicators were spreading like a disease through Meridian's once-stable structure. The station was dying, its demise accelerated by forces no one had fully understood or anticipated.

In a way, it was fitting—Meridian had been built to study and harness the deorum ore, and now it was being destroyed by the very power it had sought to control. A lesson, perhaps, in the dangers of reaching too far, too fast.

But lessons were for historians, and Voss was concerned only with the present crisis. The child had to be found. The power it represented could not be allowed to slip through Praetorium's grasp, nor could it fall into the hands of whoever had sent the android to assist the Langleys.

"Ma'am," one of the android technicians called out, "I'm picking up an energy reading. Faint, but distinctive. Section 5-C, Level 4."

"Send all available teams," Voss said. "And prepare my ship for immediate departure. I'll lead the extraction personally."

10

BORN INTO THE FIRE

In the hidden medical room, alarms blared as Cira's vital signs flatlined. Dalen clutched her hand, his face contorted with anguish as he watched the woman he loved slip away before his eyes.

"Do something!" he pleaded to Sern, who worked, administering emergency treatments and monitoring vital functions. "Save her!"

"No response to resuscitation attempts," Sern said, his voice maintaining that unnervingly even tone despite the crisis. "Deorum energy depletion has caused irreversible cellular breakdown. Dalen. She is gone."

The newborn wailed from her makeshift crib—a supply case that Sern had adapted. Her cries seemed to intensify as if sensing her mother's passing, a sound of pure loss that echoed Dalen's own shattered heart.

"No," he whispered, pressing his forehead against Cira's still-warm hand. "Please, god, no, not after all this, not now, we need you, the girls need you, I need you."

Dalen's world collapsed into a singular point of grief. The station's warning klaxons, the shuddering walls, the distant explosions—all faded to white noise against the deafening silence of Cira's heart.

Dalen's throat constricted as reality crashed over him. Her hand was still warm but utterly still. The monitors' flat tone. His daughter's cries pierced all, manifesting within this single moment.

How could the universe demand this price? Everything they'd sacrificed, every risk calculated—none of it had prepared him for this emptiness swallowing him whole.

Twenty years of memories cascaded through him. Their first meeting in the research commons. Her laugh when he'd spilt coffee across his presentation notes. The way she'd touched his face the night he proposed, fingers trembling with something more profound than happiness. Their whispered dreams of changing worlds. The arguments over ethical boundaries that somehow always ended with them holding each other, united despite their differences.

The birth of their first daughter. The terror and wonder of becoming parents.

And now this—their second child born into loss, Cira's final gift delivered at the cost of her own life.

"Dalen, we have structural failure in adjacent sections." Sern's voice barely penetrated his consciousness. "We must relocate."

The baby's cries pierced through his stupor. His daughter—their daughter—needed him. How could he possibly be enough without Cira? How could anyone navigate this universe alone? He didn't know, but he would have to work it out for his girls.

The station groaned, metal twisting somewhere nearby. But Dalen couldn't move, couldn't release Cira's cooling hand, couldn't accept that their story ended here.

Another violent tremor shook the room, and more ceiling panels crashed down around them. The station was coming apart faster now, the initial breach having weakened critical support structures throughout Meridian's central core.

"We must evacuate now," Sern said, moving to secure the newborn. "Station structural integrity has fallen below sustainable levels. Complete collapse imminent."

"I can't leave her," Dalen protested, still clutching Cira's lifeless hand.

"The child requires protection," Sern said, his logic cutting through Dalen's grief. "Your wife's sacrifice will be meaningless if her daughter falls into Praetorium's hands—or perishes with the station."

The harsh truth of those words stirred something within Dalen. He looked from Cira's peaceful face to the tiny infant Sern was wrapping in thermal blankets. His daughter. Their daughter. The miracle Cira had given her life to bring into the world.

He reached out to touch Cira's face one last time, committing every detail to memory. "I'll protect her," he promised. "With everything I have. For both of us."

Another explosion rocked the station, this one close enough to blow out the room's remaining intact panels. Warning klaxons blared with renewed urgency:

"Critical structural failure in progress. Estimated time to complete station collapse: twelve minutes. All remaining personnel proceed to emergency escape pods immediately."

"We must go," Sern said, the newborn now secured in a makeshift carrier attached to his chest. "Our exit route will be compromised within minutes."

Dalen pressed a final kiss to Cira's forehead, then forced himself to his feet. Every step away from her felt like tearing out a piece of his soul, but the cries of his daughter pulled him forward, giving him purpose amid the devastating loss.

They moved into the corridor, where the destruction was even more apparent. Entire sections of the ceiling had collapsed, walls were buckled and twisted, and sparking conduits dangled like wounded serpents from exposed infrastructure. The air was growing thin as life support systems failed throughout the station.

"This way," Sern directed, leading them toward what had once been a maintenance shaft but was now partially crushed by the station's ongoing collapse. "The primary evacuation routes are not viable. We must use alternative means."

They worked their way through the dying station, each step a battle against both the physical destruction and the emotional devastation threatening to overwhelm Dalen. The only thing keeping him moving was the tiny life Sern carried—the last piece of Cira, the future they had dreamed of together.

As they rounded a corner, they came face to face with a Praetorium security team—three officers in tactical gear, weapons raised.

"Halt!" the lead officer said. "By order of Dr. Voss, surrender the child right now!"

Sern's reaction was instantaneous. He pushed Dalen behind a collapsed support beam, shielding the baby with his body as the security team opened fire. Pulse rounds impacted Sern's frame, tearing through his exterior shell to reveal the complex mechanisms beneath.

"When I engage them, proceed to junction point C-7," Sern instructed Dalen, his voice now distorted by damage to his vocal systems. "There is a surface transport there that will take us to my ship."

"What about you?" Dalen asked, knowing the answer but needing to hear it.

"I will delay them. Then follow." Sern's damaged face turned toward him. "The child must survive. She is more important than any of us understand."

Before Dalen could protest, Sern handed him the baby carrier, securing it to Dalen's chest. Then he launched himself at the security team.

Dalen didn't wait to see the outcome. Clutching his daughter close, he ran in the direction Sern had indicated, pure panic got him through increasingly unstable corridors as Meridian continued to tear itself apart around them.

Junction point C-7 proved to be a small, unmarked access hatch near what had once been a secondary research lab. Dalen keyed it open, revealing a narrow passage beyond that led to a small, private docking port.

As Dalen entered junction point C-7, the small lunar transport vehicle waited like a beacon of salvation. Sleek and compact, it represented their last chance at escape from the dying station. He moved toward it with desperate steps, the baby carrier secured tightly against his chest.

"Freeze."

The single word sliced through the air. Dalen's blood turned to ice, the hair on his arms standing on end. He knew that voice—clinical, controlled, ruthless.

"Turn around, Langley."

Dalen pivoted slowly, curving his body to shield the infant. Emilia Voss stood ten meters away, her slender frame silhouetted against the emergency lights. The blaster in her hand remained aimed at his head.

"The child doesn't belong to you anymore," Voss said, her voice eerily calm amid the station's death throes. "Put the baby down on the ground and step back."

Dalen tightened his grip on the case. "No."

"This isn't a negotiation. That child is Praetorium property."

"Property? Fuck you. She's my daughter."

Voss's expression didn't change. "She's the culmination of years of research. The perfect subject—we knew exposing the station to unrefined deorum energy might produce some candidates down the line, we didn't expect to get this. This is a huge bonus, worth sacrificing the other potential candidates for."

The station groaned around them, another support beam giving way somewhere nearby. Dust rained from the ceiling.

"You killed Cira," Dalen said, the words almost not making it past the knot in his throat. "You wanted to expose everyone on this station to see if it would yield you more subjects, you're a fucking monster."

"The good doctor's contribution to science will be remembered. Her genetic material has been preserved." Voss took a step closer. "Now put the baby down."

Dalen shifted his weight, trying to work out if he could make it to the transport before she took the shot the distance to the transport.

"You're not thinking clearly, Dalen. This station has less than five minutes before complete structural failure. That child represents the future of humanity's relationship with deorum energy. The next evolutionary step."

Another violent tremor shook the room. A ceiling panel crashed down between them, forcing Voss to step back.

"You mean a weapon," Dalen countered. "A tool for the Praetorium to maintain control."

A bitter laugh escapes her lips. "I mean survival, Langley. Something your sentimentality will never allow for." *Her eyes narrow.* "Now give me the child, or die with the rest of this station's failures."

The baby stirred against Dalen's chest, making soft mewling sounds. He placed a protective hand over her.

"Better that than whatever you have planned for her."

Voss's eyes narrowed. "Final warning. Put. The. Child. Down."

"I won't."

"Then you'll die here, and I'll take her anyway."

The standoff stretched between them, seconds ticking away as Meridian continued to disintegrate around them. Through the viewport behind Voss, Dalen could see pieces of the station's outer ring breaking away.

"She'll never be what you want," Dalen said. "Even if you kill me, even if you take her—she's not just an experiment. She's Cira's daughter. My daughter."

"Sentiment." Voss spat the word. "That's always been your weakness. You and your wife both—brilliant minds crippled by emotion."

Another section of the ceiling collapsed. The station's automated voice announced: "Critical failure imminent. Three minutes to complete structural collapse."

"You're out of time, Dalen." Voss adjusted her grip on the blaster. "The child comes with me, one way or another."

Movement caught Dalen's eye—a shadow shifting in the corridor behind Voss. Hope surged through him.

The shadow behind Voss solidified—Sern, damaged but functional, moving as slowly as he could manage so as to not alert Voss to his presence.

"Enough games," Voss snapped, finger tightening on the trigger. "Last chance."

"You'll never understand what we created here," Dalen said, his voice steady despite the terror coursing through him. "It was never about power or control. It was about connection."

Voss's patience snapped. "Your idealism dies with you. And the child comes with me."

"She has a name."

"What?"

"My daughter. Her name is..."

The blaster discharged. Dalen felt the searing heat as the pulse round tore through his skull. His last conscious thought was of Cira's smile, of the weight of his daughter against his chest.

In the fractional second between Voss firing and Dalen's body beginning to fall, Sern launched forward with impossible speed. The station lurched, as if it were about to come out of the ground.

Voss staggered, her attention split between the collapsing ceiling and the falling infant carrier. She lunged for the baby as Sern did the same, both converging on the tiny bundle that had slipped from Dalen's lifeless grasp.

The station's main power core detonated. A blinding flash of energy surged through the corridors. The ceiling collapsed, massive support beams crashing down as the artificial gravity failed.

In that final moment of chaos—with Dalen's body crumpled on the floor, with Voss and Sern both diving for the infant, with the station tearing itself apart around them—everything dissolved into dust and blackness.

The last sound was a baby's scream, swallowed by the vacuum of space as Meridian Station ceased to exist.

11

THE QUIET DIVIDE

Golden light sliced through the darkness like a scalpel through skin. Sern's optical sensors recalibrated, adjusting to the impossible physics unfolding before him. Where there should have been nothing but vacuum and death, a sphere of shimmering energy encased them. Debris that should have crushed them hung suspended at the barrier's edge, frozen in mid-trajectory.

Sern picked himself up, his damaged left arm almost hanging loose, several servos whining with the effort. The station had disintegrated around them, yet here they were, enclosed in a pocket of atmosphere. At the centre of the sphere, the baby hovered six inches above what remained of the floor plating, tiny arms outstretched, face scrunched in concentration.

"Interesting," Sern said, head tilted as he analysed the phenomenon. "The little one has cognitive awareness beyond her time." He recorded the event in his internal log, documenting wavelength patterns and energy signatures.

Outside their golden bubble, what remained of Meridian Station drifted into the void, metal fragments spinning away like leaves in a hurricane. The sphere itself remained stationary, anchored to some fixed point in space that Sern couldn't identify.

Emilia Voss hung suspended three feet away, trapped in the same golden light that saved them. Unlike Sern and the child, she couldn't move. Her eyes, however, remained active, darting between Sern, the baby, and the void beyond. Those eyes told a story more complex than words could convey: shock at being alive, wonder at the impossible energy field, and something deeper that Sern recognised as regret. The kind of regret that comes when your entire worldview shatters in an instant.

Sern moved toward the baby, his feet finding purchase on the bubble's floor as if gravity still functioned normally. "Hello, little one," he said. "Your father entrusted you to me."

The baby's eyes opened—dark with that golden sheen, alert eyes that fixed on Sern with unnerving focus. For 2.3 seconds, Sern felt something probe his neural network, a presence light as a feather but unmistakable.

He reached for the case that had been secured to Dalen's chest. It too hung suspended, the straps drifting like seaweed in an ocean current. Sern opened the case and gently lifted the baby from her position in mid-air.

"We need to leave now," he said to her, as if she could understand. Perhaps she could.

As Sern turned toward the edge of the sphere with her secured in the case, he glanced back at Voss. Her eyes had changed again—now they held naked fear. She knew what would happen when the bubble collapsed.

"Your theories were correct," Sern said. "But your methods were flawed. This child isn't a weapon. She's something else."

Sern stepped through the edge of the sphere. The moment he crossed the threshold with her, the golden energy contracted sharply, following them like a second skin. It clung to them as Sern loaded them into the transport vehicle and onto the edge of the bubble.

Sern didn't look back. His focus narrowed to his ship, and the precious cargo sat next to him. In the vacuum of space, with no protective suit, Voss's body convulsed. The oxygen in her lungs expanded. Ice crystals formed instantly on her exposed skin. Her mouth opened in a silent scream as she drifted slowly away from the wreckage, arms outstretched toward Sern and the child, consciousness fading as the void claimed her.

* * *

The ship's hull bore the scars of Meridian's demise—impact dents and scorch marks covered the port side, and the comms array had been sheared off. Sern manipulated the external panel as best he could with one arm, and the airlock cycled open with a wheeze of struggling hydraulics.

Inside, emergency lighting bathed the cramped space in red. Sern secured the child's case to the acceleration couch, checking twice that the straps would hold. The ship's systems came online sluggishly when he initiated the startup sequence.

"Life support functional. Propulsion at sixty-three per cent capacity. Navigation systems offline,' the ship's computer announced in a flat voice.

Sern ran diagnostics while the engines warmed. The golden energy field had dissipated once they were inside the pod, leaving no trace of its existence except in Sern's memory banks. The child slept now, her tiny chest rising and falling in the rhythm of deep slumber.

"Let's get you home, little one," Sern said. "No more can be done now."

The navigation system was beyond repair, but Sern's internal positioning algorithms would suffice. They needed to reach Sacramentum's surface, it was as far as what was left of his ship would make it.

The hull shuddered as thrusters engaged. Through the viewport, Sacramentum loomed large—a yellow jewel suspended in blackness. Sern plotted a descent trajectory, compensating for the damaged stabilisers.

While the autopilot took over, Sern reached into a compartment beneath the pilot's seat. From it, he withdrew a small gold locket on a fine chain. Simple in design, it would draw no attention—just another piece of jewellery to most observers. But inside, was a deorum-dampening emitter and encoded in quantum-etched nanoscale patterns was a message that would activate if the deorum energy release was big enough.

Sern opened the child's case and placed the locket beside her. It contained a single message, "Find Lyra. She will help you." He could only hope she was still down there somewhere.

The pod's computer chimed a warning. "Atmospheric entry in sixty seconds. Structural integrity compromised. Recommend abort."

"Override," Sern said. "Continue descent."

The first tremors of reentry vibrated through the hull. Sern placed a protective hand over the case as the ship began to shake to the point that he knew it wouldn't hold together. Outside, plasma streaked past the viewport as they punched through Sacramentum's upper atmosphere.

Sern knew the chances of survival were suboptimal. But they had no alternative. He needed to get the child back to the only family she had left, her sister.

If they survived landing.

"Thirty seconds to surface," the computer announced as warning lights flashed across the console.

Sern's processors ran probability calculations. The ship's heat shield was failing. The stabilisers couldn't compensate for their spin. Impact would exceed safety parameters by at least 300%.

He looked down at the child, unaware of what was happening around her, still somehow sleeping through the chaos. In that moment, something shifted in Sern's priority matrix. His original programming emphasised self-preservation as a primary directive. But now, protecting this child overrode everything else.

Sern detached himself from the pilot's seat and wrapped his body around the child's case, using his frame as an additional buffer. It wasn't enough. It wouldn't be enough. Unless...

Sern spoke to the sleeping child, his algorithm and programming computed that the child wouldn't understand, but the android was out of options. "I must ask for your assistance once more. The ship is breaking apart, and I cannot land us safely."

For a long moment, nothing happened. Sern's calculations had anticipated this outcome—the child's power had manifested in crisis, not by request. The ground rushed toward them, trees and rocky outcroppings growing larger by the second.

"I apologise, little one. My function was to protect you, and I have failed." Sern tightened his grip around the case, metal arms forming a protective cage. His voice modulator softened to a gentle hum. "Your sister would have been proud of your strength today."

The ship's hull screamed as it tore apart. Sern's final action was to position himself between the child and the approaching ground, his processors accepting termination as the price of her survival.

Sern tightened his grip on the case. "I will protect you," he promised as the world outside became fire and sound.

The desert floor filled the viewport, close enough now to make out individual rocks and sand dunes. Close enough to count the seconds until impact.

Metal screamed as the shuttle's hull compressed beyond all engineering tolerances. The viewport spider-webbed, then exploded inward in a shower of crystalline fragments. Fire bloomed through the cabin as fuel lines ruptured, the roar of flames mixing with the shriek of tearing bulkheads. The deck bucked upward, throwing bodies against the ceiling before gravity slammed them down again into twisted wreckage.

A flash of golden light pulsed once across the wasteland, brighter than the twin suns, visible from orbit.

Then nothing.

Dedicated to Mason & Rupert,
you'll forever be my inspiration.
– Dad

**Check out more titles at
www.astraechoes.co.uk**

IF YOU READ THIS AND ENJOYED IT!!

PLEASE DROP ME A FOLLOW, AND TAG US ON INSTAGRAM

@ ASTRA ECHOES

THANKS

G. ORON

www.ingramcontent.com/pod-product-compliance
Ingram Content Group UK Ltd.
Pitfield, Milton Keynes, MK11 3LW, UK
UKHW041907120226
467964UK00002B/5